GUARDI

Dreams

Can the end be the only beginning?

By:
Ashley Marie Sweet

To: All ob Grandma's
Kids!
I hope you
enjoy this!! :)
-Ashley Sweet

Published by TripleSweet Morgans

Printed in the United States of America

Cover Design: Eva and Ed Sweet

Direct Inquiries to:
TripleSweetMorgans@hotmail.com
www.TripleSweetMorgans.com

ISBN 1-4276-0907-1

9 781427 609076

50995

Dedicated to:

Mary Elizabeth Anthony
For her love and compassion
toward horses and the
magnificent breed called
Friesians.

Thanks to all who made this book possible.
You're the Best!

March 2006

PROLOGUE

The big Friesian mare got to her feet and looked down at her little newborn foal. "Easy girl, easy Violet," said Heather as she knelt down beside the foal. "It's a colt," she said as she began to rub down the foal. As they sat there, Heather remembered the night Violet was born. She remembered sitting there as Violet took her first breath 12 years ago. Now she sat there watching Violet's foal take his first breath.

Suddenly Violet started to pace and get stressed as if something was going on or about to happen. "What's wrong girl?" asked Heather, but she no sooner got the words out of her mouth, when Violet stumbled to the ground. And as fast as she foaled the first time, she foaled again. Heather was excited and scared, mares that have twins usually kick one away. This foal was even smaller than the colt. Even though females were smaller than males, this filly was way too small.

Heather jumped up and ran out of the stall, down the aisle, and into the tack room. She grabbed another towel and a pail of bran mash. She carefully and quietly went back down the barn aisle and back into the stall. Violet was on her feet, and instead of cleaning the filly she was cleaning the colt. Heather set the bran down and as Violet ran to eat it, the colt tried to get up and follow. After a few tries he staggered to his feet and began to nurse.

Heather turned her attention to the little filly that lay in the corner of the stall. She picked up the towel and went over to the filly and started to rub her dry. The little filly sat there in the warmth of the stall. After a few minutes, the filly began to move around and get a feel for where she was. Heather sat there, hoping the filly would climb to her feet. When the filly didn't, she got up and ran to the stable office to call the vet.

"Twins?!" the vet said in alarm.

"Yes twins. The colt that was born first is on his feet and looks healthy. But the filly that was born about an hour ago, isn't even trying to get on her feet," explained Heather in a worried voice.

"I'll be over there in 15 minutes," the vet said before hanging up.

Heather threw the phone down and ran to the house. She burst through the door, only to see her father grabbing his coat from the hook.

"What's going on out there?" he said in his gruff voice. "The barn's not that far from the house you know. I still can hear the sounds of stressed horses."

"Sorry, but," Heather started.

"But nothing. How's Violet?" he demanded.

"Violet had twins," she answered, "one of them doesn't seem okay. I already called the vet."

They both stood there in awe for a moment, taking in what was happening. She pushed a strand of brown hair away from her face. The silence was broken by the sound of a car.

"The vet's here," she said turning and running down the short path that led to the barn. Kurt Lutgens, the stable's vet, jumped out and ran to the barn with Heather at his side.

"How has she been?" he said as they headed for Violet's stall.

"Violet was fine when I left the stall. I just told father," she said in a rush.

As they came to the stall, Violet was finishing her bran mash and the colt was sleeping at her feet. The little filly was still at the back of the stall lying in the straw, motionless. They went into the stall without a word. Kurt looked at Violet quick, and then turned to the filly that now had her head in Heather's lap. Kurt examined the filly carefully, and then looked at Heather; his eyes filled with as much worry as hers.

"Hold her still," Kurt said pulling a container and needle from his bag. Heather did as she was told and held the filly in a firm grasp. He injected the liquid into the little Friesian filly, and then looked at Heather.

"She might not make it Heather," Kurt said putting a hand on her shoulder.

Before she had a chance to respond, she once again heard her father's gruff voice, "How is it?"

They both looked up.

"It's pretty sick, and it won't make it without intensive care," Kurt explained.

"Well, do away with it then," he said heartlessly.

"No!! Father, please give her a chance. Please?!" exclaimed Heather, horrified at the thought of putting the little filly to sleep. This was quite a remark for a 17-year-old girl to say to someone like her father.

"End her misery before it starts," he said looking at Kurt.

Heather was now on her feet and in front of her father. She looked him straight in the eye, "Father, please, give the foal a chance."

"You do not talk to me like that young lady!" Jake stormed.

"Jake, the foal will have a good chance if she gets milk." Kurt said, also trying to save the foal's life, "But it might take a bottle or a nanny goat, because Violet has already pushed her away."

"I'll take care of her," Heather blurted out.

"You'll do no such thing. You're going to boarding school after the remark you made," Jake said angrily.

"I have a couple nanny goats. I could, sort of, lend you one. No cost either," Kurt said trying to save the foal in any way possible.

"Okay. If somebody you know will be willing to take care of the two," replied Jake.

After thinking a minute Kurt answered, "I'm sure my niece would, she loves caring for foals. And she just got out of college and is looking for a job,"

"Well she'll be at the lowest of minimum wage, because I'm not looking to give it away as a job in the first place," Jake snapped back.

After agreeing on a wage, Kurt called his niece, who jumped at the thought of taking care of the foal, and said she didn't care how much the pay was. All the while, Heather sat at the foal's side. She was relieved that her father let it live, but disappointed she wouldn't be at the foal's side through her recovery.

Heather couldn't believe that her father was sending her to boarding school just because she talked back to him. Her father in general was a mean brute; he'd been like that ever since she could remember. Her mother had died 2 years ago, but that didn't change him one bit. Some fathers just say things to get kids to calm down or to get them out of the way, but her father always meant what he said.

"I wish I could stay to help you, but father is sending me away," whispered Heather as she lay at the filly's side. "I guess angels were watching over you tonight," that sparked an idea for Heather, "Your name will be Angel. Welcome to the world Angel."

∪∪∪

If only everything would be as comforting as Heather's words. Unfortunately, nothing seemed to be for Angel. Kurt's niece Karen came to feed her every day, but it didn't seem the same. Then, just when they came to trust each other, Jake put her in her own stall and sent Karen off looking for a different job. Now nobody was there to stand by Angel. Nobody. So months rolled on, barn hands were told only to clean her stall in their free time (which they didn't have much of). Then came the worst part, training with Jake.

Jake trained most of the horses himself. He decided he would train Angel. Except for Heather, everyone called her Nag or some other bad name. For a whole five years Angel was beaten if she didn't or just wasn't able to do something right. Then Jake discovered something, Angel or Nag, had a star on her forehead. Jake was going crazy. Friesians were supposed to be totally black.

"That's it!!!" he screamed to some of the barn hands, "That horse is being sold at the next auction. The thing shoulda' been put to sleep the night it was born. Star on its forehead, can't walk straight, kicks holes in the wall. It's unbelievable; it's being sold at the next auction around here!"

THE AUCTION

As Liz drove down the road, she couldn't stop thinking about the horse she might get; Mary Elizabeth Parker (Liz) was a 34-year-old Irish woman who lived in north Scranton, Pennsylvania. Her parents passed away two years before. Even though she missed them, she put herself to work in doing something she couldn't have done before. She turned her father's old construction barn into a seven-stall stable. Now she was going to the auction to maybe get a horse to put into it. She loved all horses, but she loved Friesians the best. She knew that Friesians cost more than the average horse, and she told herself that she wouldn't bid any more than $3,000.

It seemed like an eternity, but she finally reached the auction house. She found a parking spot and made sure everything in the trailer was okay before going inside the huge building. She picked up a brochure as she came through the door. There, she found hundreds of stockade pens filled with horses. Horses of all different shapes, colors and personalities. As she walked from pen to pen, she asked questions about each one. She wished she could take all of them home, but she picked four that she thought would fit her lifestyle. Some were flashy, piped up show horses, but she wasn't planning on showing. Some were carriage horses, but she was looking for a good riding horse. There were some of the cutest foals, but she wasn't looking for a training project either. So she came down to the four she thought would be best.

The bay Mustang gelding, Rocky; an Appaloosa mare, Dixie; a black Thoroughbred gelding, Spike; and a tobino Paint mare named, Hilda. Liz was a little disappointed that she didn't see any Friesians for sale.

"Ladies and gentlemen please take your seats, the bidding will begin in seven minutes," boomed the loud speaker. "Finally," Liz said as she found a seat in the second row. The bidding started up, horses started going for more and more as the bidding went on. Liz was hoping the horses she had picked out wouldn't go for as much as the others did. Unfortunately, they went for just as much. Dixie went for $4,200, Hilda went for $4,000, and Spike went for $3,700. It wasn't over though, Rocky, the Mustang, hadn't gone yet.

"And here we have about a 10 year old Mustang, straight from the Wild's of Montana; he's been handled for 6 years and has been gelded. Responds to the name Rocky. Now, who will give me $600?!!" said the auctioneer in a loud voice.

"$700!!" Liz yelled.

"I got $700, do I hear $800?" he went on.

"$1,000!" somebody yelled from the back.

Liz didn't give the auctioneer a chance, "$1,500!!"

"Okay then, do I hear a higher bid?" asked the auctioneer, "Going, going, sold to the woman in the second row! You may see and pick up your horse at the end of the auction, ma'am."

Liz couldn't believe it; she'd actually bought a horse. The next 15 horses went by in a whirl. Then it was the last horse. The man walked in with a mare that looked like it'd been living in manure and mud all its life. The mare was a sight of flashing hooves and bared teeth.

The mare showed the whites of her eyes in fear. Her coat was a mess of matted hair and dried mud.

"And here is a Friesian mare, uh.... um, unnamed and green to the saddle," the auctioneer said in a confused voice.

Liz's heart went out to the mare. A purebred Friesian mare, neglected for whatever reason. Her thoughts were broken by the auctioneer's loud, booming voice, "Do I hear $400?"

There was silence. "$300?......$200?"

"$50 for dog meat!" came a voice from the back.

"Going, going..."

"$55 to a good home!!!!" Liz screamed in her loudest voice.

"All right, is there a higher bid?" everybody was silent again.

"Going, going, sold! To the woman in the second row!"

Liz hadn't even realized what she just did. She only came to get one started horse. Now she was going home with two horses; a happy, in-shape one, and a neglected, scared one. But all she could think about was getting her two new horses home and settled in. She walked right up to the man and took the lead rope from his grasp.

"Well, good luck with her," he said before turning away.

"Hey!" she called after him, "Here's your $55 dollars," she said pulling the money from her pocket and slapping it into his hand. He grunted and handed her the paper work. Now Liz turned her attention to the mare. She sat there for 10 minutes, just stroking her face and murmuring soothing words. Finally the mare calmed down. That's when Liz noticed that the mare was wheezing. Liz knew she had to get this mare home and get a vet to check her.

Step, by hesitant, stiff step, Liz and the Friesian mare made it to the trailer. She tied the mare to the trailer and ripped a bail of hay open and used it as a substitute for straw to give the mare a nice cushion. After carefully loading the scared mare, she went to pick up Rocky. At that moment, she thanked God that she had a two-horse trailer with her. She found Rocky eagerly waiting to be picked up. She paid the man and signed the paper work, then looked at the lively gelding and smiled. The gelding thrusted his head into Liz's chest as she reached for the lead rope. She wished that only the Friesian mare could be as healthy as Rocky. His bay coat glistening in the summer sun, his eyes full of life.

She quickly loaded Rocky, who seemed to have no problem getting into the trailer. It was a half an hour from here to her house. She drove home slowly so as not to disturb the mare. As she drove home she called the vet, "Hi, I have a Friesian mare that I just bought at an auction and I really need some one to look at her," she said, then explained what shape the mare was in.

"Okay, I'll be right over," said the vet on the other end.

After giving him directions to her house she hung up. It seemed that she was never going to reach her house. Finally, she saw the drive that lead up to her home. This was when she told herself that the horses she'd bought were going to be fine.

THE VET VISIT

Once Liz was home and had Rocky and the Friesian mare unloaded, she went to examine both of them to make sure neither was injured by the trip. Rocky was fine, but was extremely curious, pacing his stall and snorting in excitement. Liz went to check on the mare. The Friesian she'd been dreaming of had a beautiful, thick streaming mane and tail, a silky, shiny, black coat; this mare had a bur-matted mane, and a dull mud dried coat. As Liz entered the stall, the mare retreated to the back of the stall, her whole body quivering.

"Easy girl, easy." Liz soothed as she took a step. The mare snorted and looked at her as if she'd never heard such words before. After that, the mare seemed to be willing to let her look and come closer. The mare's fetlocks were swollen, her knees were badly blistered and cut, and she was having a hard time breathing.

Liz was relieved when she heard a truck pull up in the driveway. The mare gave a shrilling whinny and reared.

"Easy girl, easy," Liz said as she backed out of the stall. She walked down the aisle and out of the barn to meet the vet.

"Hello, I'm Kurt Lutgens. Where's the mare? It sounded bad by what you said on the phone," he said shaking her hand.

"This way," Liz replied as she headed toward the barn.

15

As they came to the stall, Kurt stopped dead. "This is the mare from Jake's stable. I had no idea he was selling her," he said as if he were in a daze. He opened the door and the mare reared up once more.

"Easy now, easy," he murmured just like Liz had a few moments before. "This horse has had a very hard life," he said as he put down his bag and began getting his gloves on. "Is there a light in here?" he asked looking up at Liz

"Oh yes, hold on," she said as she swiftly headed down to the little office she'd built. It wasn't really a tack room yet; it had her old saddle, a bridle and a little desk that was cluttered with brushes and hoof picks, and two shovels and pitch fork that lay up against the wall. She flipped the switch that would turn on the stall lights, and then headed back down the aisle. As she looked in the stall, Kurt was feeling down the mare's legs, and then he felt her back, her neck and checked her gums.

"She has a type of pneumonia, and she's dehydrated," he paused as he looked at Liz. "But I can't figure out what exactly is wrong with her legs unless we bring her to the clinic. It's only 10 minutes so it won't be that long of a drive," he added seeing her worried face.

"Okay, I'll get the trailer," Liz said turning and jogging out to pull up the trailer. All she wanted was for that mare to be healthy again. Kurt, having known the man who owned her before the auction, explained to Liz that her new mare had had a hard life for the years she'd been with him. Yet Liz had to concentrate, she was going to get this mare the life it had deserved before. She pulled the trailer up, and with the help of the vet, the mare was in the trailer and on her way to the vet clinic.

For the whole 10-minute ride, Liz just prayed. Please let her be okay, please let this mare live. She gripped the wheel until her knuckles turned white. As they pulled into the driveway of the clinic, two men opened the big barn doors. She stopped and parked in the place Kurt had told her to, and jumped out and ran to the back. They pulled the ramp down, and together helped the mare out. As Liz led the mare, Kurt led the way to the stall.

"She can go right in here," he said opening the stall door.

"Easy girl, easy," they soothed as the Friesian stepped cautiously into the stall.

Almost on cue, two women and a man came in and started to work on the mare. First they gave her enough morphine to get her to lie down, then began washing off the mud, manure, and dried blood from the mare's coat.

"Come on, there's nothing you can do at this point," Kurt said putting a hand on her shoulder, "Come into the lounge, I need to tell you something."

Liz followed Kurt into the lounge. It was a clean white room with pictures of all different kinds of animals on the wall.

"Here," said Kurt handing her a cup of steaming coffee, "Sit down."

Liz took a seat on the brown leather couch and sipped her coffee.

"That mare wasn't always that way, in that kind of shape," Kurt began, "She was born a twin, and the mother chose her brother over her. Jake, the man you bought her from, wanted the filly to be put to sleep. Heather, Jake Fleming's daughter, stood up to her father, in a way that even I wouldn't have. Even though the filly was saved, Jake sent Heather off to boarding school after the remark. My daughter cared for and looked after the filly for three months. A year later, Jake thought it was time to start training," he stopped to sip his coffee, "The mare went through 5 years of beating and neglect before Jake was fed up."

"She's only five?" Liz gasped, thinking the mare was probably 15.

"Yep," he continued, "The last thing Heather did before she left, was stay in the barn for two nights, against her father's orders, and talked to the filly and massaged her until her fingers were raw, so I'm almost positive that that mare will respond to Heather."

Liz just sat there, taking everything in and thinking about how this filly must have lived.

"But here's the other part," Kurt said, breaking her thoughts.

"What do mean other part?" she questioned.

"The day Heather turned 19, she dropped out of boarding school and bought a house. She's been working on saving up to build a small stable and buy a couple of horses, and,"

"Wait, hold on, how do you know all this?" she cut him off.

"My son used to date her, and she used to come for dinner and help me with some of my calls," he answered. "My real point is, that she's right, as in directly, across the street from your place."

They sat there in silence for a moment, as Liz took in what was happening. *The girl that used to own the mare I just bought is living right across the street from me.* She thought and thought. She hadn't realized how long they had been in the lounge, until the vets that had been working on the mare came in.

"The only thing she needs now is rest. And we prefer that she stay here tonight," one woman explained, "She's in no shape to go in a trailer anyway."

"Okay. Thank you so much," Liz replied.

She headed out of the lounge and down the aisle to the mare's temporary stall. The mare was lying on the bedding of shavings. Half dazed and numb from the day's episodes, Liz just stood there, staring at the mare that was supposedly getting better.

REUNION OF LIFE

Liz only got about 2 hours of sleep that night. Her head was in a whirl from everything that she'd heard and experienced. She had to talk to Heather; she had to get Heather and the mare together. She was 99% sure that seeing Heather again would make the Friesian much, much happier. It would probably speed up the recovery if the mare had someone she knew and trusted by her side.

She took a relaxing shower, dressed, and went outside to see and feed Rocky. She felt bad for him. A beautiful Mustang, sitting in this new barn all by himself, no one seemed to be paying any attention to him. As she walked in the barn door, a happy, shrill of a whinny pierced the air.

"Hello big, beautiful, boy. How ya' doing Rocky?" she said, sliding his stall door open and patting his big muscular neck. She rubbed his neck and kissed his face before stepping out of the stall and going into the hay barn. She cut open a bail of hay and pulled three biscuits out and headed back to Rocky's stall. She threw the biscuits into the hayrack, and headed to get her brushes. She must've spent a whole hour standing there brushing and talking to him.

She told him everything that had happened the day before. She looked into Rocky's gentle, caring eyes, and she burst into tears.

"Oh Rocky," she sobbed, "I don't know what to do. I don't know what to think." She let her heavy tears roll out onto Rocky's thick, black mane. She threw her arms around Rocky's neck and continued to sob. Then she felt something push into her back and push her into Rocky's broad chest. It was Rocky, he seemed to be telling her that it was okay; he would be there for her. Liz hugged him tightly then stepped back to look at his face. "I love you Rocky. I always will. I'll always do what's best for you, I promise," she said as she kissed his face. She stood there hugging Rocky, until she finally calmed down. Standing there with him seemed to give her courage, and she then knew what she had to do. She gave Rocky a big kiss, stepped out of the stall and headed for the house. She washed her face and sat on her bed. Rocky had just seemed to tell her that no matter what happened, he was always there. She said a prayer, thanking God for the gift of the beautiful Mustang. Once she felt that God had received her prayer, she got up and went outside. She walked back to Rocky's stall and put his halter on. He sat there quietly as she fumbled with the buckle. She grabbed a lead rope and headed outside with mustang in tow.

She led him to the paddock gate and turned him loose. The back of the paddock was on a slight hill, but was okay for him to kick up his heels. The whole paddock was dotted with apple trees, but Rocky didn't seem to notice, for he stayed right along the fence line. Liz put the lead rope in the barn then headed back outside. She had to talk to Heather, she had to. As she walked down the driveway, Rocky stopped grazing, and followed her. Since the fence line lined the driveway, it was easy for him to follow. At the end of the driveway she reached through the rails and patted Rocky's neck, "Wish me luck boy."

GUARDIAN ANGEL

She walked across the street and up the sidewalk. Before she knew what she was doing, she rang the doorbell. Almost instantly, someone answered, "Hello, may I help you." A tall, slim woman appeared. Her light brown hair came down to the middle of her back. "Hi, does Heather Fleming live here?" Liz asked. "Yes. I'm Heather. May I know who you are?" she said quickly. "Elizabeth Parker. I need to talk to you," Liz responded.

In a flash, they were sitting in Heather's living room. Liz sat there, while Heather got them some drinks. "Thank you," Liz said as Heather handed her a cup of coffee. "Now, what's all this about?" Heather asked taking a seat next to her. "My vet, Kurt Lutgens, told me that you used to have a horse, a Friesian mare. Well, I just bought her from your father at an auction yesterday," Liz said, as she tried not to make a lot of commotion. "What?! You bought a horse I use to…." It seemed to strike Heather like a baseball in the head. "Angel!" she said anxiously.

Heather looked at Liz in shock. They sat there in silence for what had to be 15 minutes. *Her name's Angel*, Liz thought. "Can you take me to the vet clinic to see her?" Heather asked in an embarrassed, quivering voice. "Of course. Let's go," said Liz as she stood up. There was silence as they walked out to the car. On the way to the clinic Liz told Heather all about what had happened the day before. Heather sat there, close to tears. They pulled into the driveway and headed for the door. As they walked in, Kurt greeted them and showed them to Angel's stall.

Heather pulled open the stall door, and stood there for a moment.

"Angel?" she questioned. The mare snorted and looked up at them. "Angel?" Heather questioned once more. This time the mare tried to get to her feet. Despite her efforts the mare failed to stand. The mare then stopped and looked at Heather, and gave a weak whinny.

"Angel!" Heather cried. She knelt beside the mare and held Angel's face in her hands; like she had the night she was born. Heather sobbed and whispered things into Angel's ear.

Liz and Kurt stood side by side. Tears came to their eyes as they watched the bond return once more.

"Liz," said Kurt, Liz looked at him, "You just gave Angel one great reason to live."

Liz knew it was probably true. The mare's eyes were no longer dull, but full of love; her face that had been solemn was now full of an emotion that Liz couldn't place. And Heather's face was full of complete happiness and joy.

"I love you, Angel. I love you," they heard her say. It was a sight Liz and Kurt would never forget, it was a sight that would last forever.

An hour and a half later, Angel was actually asleep. The best sleep she'd gotten in five years. Finally, Heather got to her feet with one last kiss and exited the stall. In silence, they walked out to the car.

"Bye Kurt," Heather said quickly before getting into the car along side Liz. As they drove off, Liz wondered how much that moment had just changed Heather's life. She pulled up in front of Heather's house and got out. Liz walked up to the door with her. Once there, she nodded to Heather and turned to leave.

"Liz," Heather said, Liz turned, "Thanks for telling me about Angel. I've always felt that I let her down. I have almost locked myself completely out of the world because of it." Liz saw how lifeless Heather had probably been before. Thinking that what happened to Angel was her fault. They smiled at each other, as Liz turned and they parted ways.

Liz parked her car and walked into the house. Today was another, tiring, long day. She went into the kitchen and dug up a sandwich to have for a lunch/dinner. After eating, she went out to see Rocky. As before, he was happy to see her. He stood quietly while she hooked the lead rope to his halter, and walked by her side as she led him to the barn. She gave him hay, grain, and another thorough grooming. She once again told him about her day, and she told him what Heather said to her. After finishing up with Rocky, she went inside to get a good night's sleep.

Before going to bed, she knelt down and said a special prayer to God that Angel would be okay.

CHANGES

In the days that passed, Angel was showing signs of recovery. She got a little curious about where she was. She wanted to walk around and move more, and she found out what it was like to eat a good, healthy serving of grain and hay. After three days, Liz and Heather began walking her around outside. That was where Angel learned a lot of new things; she learned that trees weren't big monsters, that there were other things beside humans and equines that could make noises, like the birds, and cars were something that she didn't have to scare off, or be scared of. After three weeks of treatment and learning, Kurt gave the all clear, "All she needs now is love and companionship."

Liz and Heather hugged each other and Kurt, before climbing into Liz's pickup and heading home to get everything ready.

"Okay, we'll get her stall ready first and then we'll do the trailer," Liz planned as they pulled into the driveway.

"Sounds like a plan. Do you have shavings or straw?" questioned Heather as the car stopped.

"I have shavings, there in the hay barn," Liz answered as they got out of the pickup and headed for the barn. Just as they stepped into the barn, Rocky gave a nice cheerful greeting.

"So this is the Rocky that I've been hearing about, and hearing," said Heather as she stopped to scratch his bold, thick neck. Liz ran around the corner into the hay barn, which was more like two stalls combined into one. She got a wheelbarrow and started to scoop the loose shavings into it. Once it was full she brought it back to the stall beside Rocky's. Liz then went to get the shovels from the office room.

Liz and Heather soon got a routine down; Liz scooped it into the middle of the stall, and Heather pushed it around. Once done with the bedding, they made sure that the corner bucket, where Angel would eat her grain from, was okay and didn't have any sharp edges. Then Liz and Heather headed out to the trailer, which only needed about two shovels of shavings.

"That's a job well done I say," said Liz as they stood back to admire their work on the trailer.

"Yeh," agreed Heather as they turned to go inside Liz's house to rest.

They walked though the door, and as Liz went to get them sodas, Heather slumped on the couch with a sigh, "I can't wait 'til Angel comes."

"Me either," said Liz as she handed Heather a soda and sat down beside her.

"So I hear you're saving to build a stable," Liz said opening her soda.

"Well, I'm not so sure. The only reason I wanted a small stable was because I hoped I could find and buy Angel from my dad if he still had her," she said as she took a sip.

Liz looked down, a little embarrassed that she owned this horse that was so special to Heather. It was two minutes before Heather spoke and pushed away the silence, "Well, I have an idea. But it might be asking a little much."

"What?" asked Liz, curious to know.

"Well," Heather hesitated, "What if we share your stable?"

Liz looked at her, thinking that, that would be fun; they could help each other with chores, and share the horses as well.

"That's a great idea," Liz responded.

"Yah think so?" Heather questioned a bit surprised.

"Of course, we could help each other with chores, share the horses and all that fun stuff," Liz said getting excited about the idea. Liz felt like a child again. And why not? This was exciting and involved horses, and she should be able to feel like a kid again.

After discussing it a little bit more, they shook hands and said that the farm would be shared. That night they had their own little party at Heather's house; they just invited Kurt, since he was the only one who knew how special this was. Liz and Heather made a great dinner, which included a special secret recipe of pasta and corn.

"If you ladies get tired of horses, which will probably never happen, you could be cooks too," joked Kurt, as they finished.

"Hold on. I have a little something for dessert," said Heather as she went into the refrigerator. She pulled out a good size dish of apple pie.

"I must be seeing things," Kurt said as Heather put it on the table, "That's my favorite."

After everything was put away, Kurt headed for home, as well as did Liz.

"Thanks for everything Liz," Heather said as Liz headed out the door.

"No problem. See you tomorrow," Liz answered, and then walked across the street. She went into the barn and fed Rocky; but was too tired to groom him. "Sorry boy. But I'm pooped," she said patting his neck. She turned out the lights and headed inside. As she walked up the porch steps, she was thankful that the past few days weren't as heart breaking as the others.

ʊʊʊ

"Hey Angel, how are you today?" said Heather as they walked into the clinic stable the next day.

"I think she knows she's going home. She's been a little more hyper and excited today," explained Kurt as he slipped a halter over the mare's head and walked her out of the stall.

"She's just smart that's all," boasted Liz as they lead the frisky mare through the barn door.

"Easy girl, easy," said Kurt as Angel started to prance about and get excited, "You guys want to put the trailer ramp down? I'm gonna walk her a bit first."

Liz and Heather walked over to the trailer, put the ramp down and slid two biscuits of hay into a net and hung it on the hook.

"That should do it," said Heather as they jumped down from the trailer and walked back over to where Kurt was walking Angel.

"Everything's set," Liz told Kurt.

"Okay, she's all yours," Kurt smiled as he handed Liz the lead.

"Let's go home girl," Liz said, taking the lead rope from Kurt. Liz eased Angel into the trailer, said good-bye to Kurt, then jumped in beside Heather and drove off. She sat there as Heather steered the pickup down the road toward the ranch.

As they pulled into the driveway, Angel told them she was ready to come out of the trailer. Heather pulled the truck to a stop, and they both jumped out and ran around to the back of the trailer.

"Calm down girl. You're all right," they soothed as they let the ramp down. Liz walked around and climbed in the door that was toward the front that allowed a person to get into the trailer and be by the horse's head. She took hold of Angel's halter and clipped a lead rope to it.

"Good girl, now back up. Come on, back up," Liz coaxed as Angel carefully took small steps backward. After a few minutes, Angel was out of the trailer and looking around.

Liz and Heather carefully led Angel into the barn, and into her new stall. Rocky was more than happy to see a new horse and whinnied a cheerful greeting. Angel whinnied back in response, and pushed her nose through the bars that separated the stall. Liz and Heather stayed around the barn most of the day making sure Angel was settling in okay. Night came and they fed both horses, and gave them a good grooming. Once Liz and Heather were out of the stalls and everything was put away, they went to say goodnight. They came to Angel's stall to see her nose to nose with Rocky. They smiled at each other and turned out the light.

THE ACCIDENT

As days turned into weeks, Angel started to become more and more comfortable with everything around her. She and Rocky could trot around the paddock for the longest time. A month had gone by, and Liz and Heather started to work her on the lunge-line. At first Angel thought if she ran in fast circles she could get away from the long winding rope, but after several failed attempts, she got the point that the rope wasn't getting nearly as tired or dizzy as she was. Soon, Heather started working her in long-lines, while Liz started working Rocky in them.

After a month of working with the horses, Liz and Heather gave them a break and put them out to pasture. The splitting of the barn and chores worked out very well. Liz did Rocky's stall, while Heather did Angel's. They each chipped in for the hay and grain, along with shavings, and grass seed for the pasture.

One day Heather announced that she had to go see her grandmother. It was her birthday and she was going to the family party.

"That's great. You need a break anyway," Liz replied.

"You're sure you don't mind cleaning up around here by yourself?" Heather questioned wanting to make sure it would be all right.

"We only have two horses; it's not that big a deal. Really," assured Liz.

"Okay. Well if you need anything just call, I'm only an hour away and I've got my cell-phone with me," Heather said not wanting to leave Liz to do everything on her own.

"I'll be fine. You go and have a good time," Liz said giving Heather a hug.

"Bye," shouted Heather, as she got into the car. Liz waved her off, and then headed into the barn to clean the stalls. Heather had already put Rocky and Angel out so all she had to do was get down to work. She cleaned the stalls in a zip, filled the hay nets, and washed the buckets and filled them. She ran a hand across her forehead and sat down on a hay bale.

It was about noontime so she went to the house and made herself a salad. She sat on the couch and watched TV for a while, just taking a rest. After finishing her salad, she put her plate in the sink and walked back outside. She stood on the porch for a minute and watched as Rocky and Angel played a game of tag. She walked down to the fence line and pulled two carrots from her pocket, "Here guys, come and get it!" she called, sticking her hand through the fence. The two horses looked in her direction and came racing down from the far end of the pasture at a dead gallop. You would never think that just two months ago Angel had been an underfed, dehydrated mare. They snatched their carrots and gobbled them up in a flash.

She rubbed each of their faces, and then headed for the barn. She still had to sweep the aisle and rake out the hay barn, which had been filled yesterday. Liz picked up a broom and just swept and raked until her arms felt like they were going to fall off. After dumping the last load of old hay into the manure pile and putting her cleaning utensils back in place, she once again slumped onto a bale of hay. Liz sat there for a minute or two, just catching her breath. She realized what a good team her and Heather were on a daily basis.

She gave a sigh and went to bring Rocky and Angel inside for the night. She hadn't realized how quick the day had gone by; it was about 4:20pm. She walked outside and up to the gate. Angel was always brought in first, she was the boss. Angel walked up to the gate and allowed Liz to hook her to the lead. Once Angel was in her stall and eating her grain, Liz went out to bring in Rocky, who went through almost the same routine as Angel did, prance out and then quietly walk to the barn. She wouldn't be able to groom them tonight, she was too tired. So she turned out the lights and headed to the house.

She no sooner got her shoes off, than did the phone ring, "Hello, is M. Elizabeth Parker there?" questioned a man on the other end.

"Speaking. Who is this?" Liz replied.

"There has been a car accident involving a girl whom you know to be Heather Fleming. We are sorry to inform you that she did not survive the accident," the man said quickly.

"What?" Liz said in shock. Heather just died in a car crash? Everything was happening too fast.

"Ma'am?" the man questioned.

"Oh, thank you for calling me sir," was all Liz could say before she hung up. She ran to her bedroom and flopped on her bed and began to sob. She cried herself to sleep, not even bothering to change out of her jeans and sweatshirt.

"Why!? Why!?" she screamed all night, "Why me Lord! Why me!"

She cried and cried until her body seemed to run out of tears.

∪∪∪

Soon, morning was here. Liz got up and took a long hot shower and tried to relax. But no matter what she did, she couldn't stop crying. She went outside to see two confused horses. She stumbled into Angel's stall and wrapped her arms around her thick neck and continued to sob. "She's gone Angel. Heather's gone." Angel stood there, her eyes full of sympathy. Liz kissed her face and hugged her tight. Rocky stood there and nickered gently, as he was confused at the sight he was seeing.

They all stood there in silence for the longest of time. She went into Rocky's stall and did the same thing she'd done with Angel. Once she'd calmed down a little she gave each of them a final pat and went back in the house. She walked over and picked up the phone and called Kurt.

"I'm so sorry Liz. Are you gonna' be okay or do you want me to come over and take care of the horses?" he asked after she'd explained what happened.

"I'll be okay. It's just that she was so young and, and….," she cut herself off to hold back tears. "Um, I need to go, I'll talk to you later," Liz said quickly before hanging up. She picked up the phone again to find out where Heather was.

∪∪∪

"We pray that our friend will rest peacefully. We will never forget Heather, may she always be in our hearts," the priest spoke at the funeral. Liz stepped forward and laid a bouquet of Lilies and a picture of Angel at Heather's side.

"I love you," she whispered before stepping back to let the rest of Heather's family and friends lay their gifts in the casket. Liz couldn't sit there any longer; she said good-bye to Kurt and headed out to her car. She climbed in and drove off without a second glance.

Once home she brought in Angel and Rocky, fed them and gave them a good long grooming. "What would I be without you two?" she said as she groomed out their dark silky manes and tails. After spending two and a half months with Heather at her side, it was going to be a big change for Liz, Rocky, and Angel. "Okay, tomorrow I am going to get hay and shavings. So I'll have to clean out the back of the pickup," Liz talked to herself as she finished feeding Rocky and Angel. She closed the grain can lids, grabbed a broom and headed outside.

The back of the pickup was cluttered with the hay and shavings from the last trip. Liz sighed and began to sweep out the bed of the pickup.

"That should do it," she said as she climbed off the bed of the pickup. "Now to get a good night's rest," she yawned as she put the broom in the barn and turned out the lights. Once inside she washed her face, changed into her pajamas and slid into bed after saying her prayers, "Thank you for this day and keep all of us in your hearts. Amen." She crossed herself and laid down. Before she knew what was happening, she was sound asleep.

STARTING OVER

Liz soon found a routine that would fit her new life; the stalls were mucked out on Monday, Wednesday, and Saturday. Then she picked up hay and shaving every other Thursday. Saturday and Tuesday were cleaning and/or training days. Kurt came over to help in between calls, but he knew she had it pretty much under control. Although the first week and a half she was extremely tired all the time.

One day Kurt pulled into the driveway and came walking up with an envelope in his hand, "Here, this is from Heather's grandmother," he said holding out the envelope. Liz slowly put down her mucking shovel and took the envelope from Kurt. She opened it up to find a note and a check. Before saying anything, she read the note:

Dear Liz,

Heather had told me all about what you guys were doing. She said how you agreed to share your ranch, along with everything in it. The family had agreed to split the money in her bank account, and I think you deserve as good a share as anybody. You wouldn't have believed how down she always was before she met you and found Angel again. So the family thanks you very much.

With Love,
Amelia Bolton

Liz looked at Kurt and smiled, she was surprised at how much Heather had told her grandmother, and surprised that it meant so much to them. After showing the note to Kurt, they went inside for a drink.

"I never realized how much it meant to them," explained Liz as they sat out on the porch.

"You'd be surprised," answered Kurt.

"Here you go," said Liz as they came back onto the porch, and she handed Kurt a glass of ice-tea.

"Thank you," Kurt responded taking the glass.

"How's everything been around here?" he asked taking a sip.

"Good. We've been a little down, but we're hanging in there," said Liz before taking a sip of hers.

After finishing their ice-tea, both Liz and Kurt went back to work. Liz went to the barn and picked up her shovel and continued to muck out Rocky's stall. Once Rocky's was done she quickly did Angel's, then headed out to the pasture to see them.

"Here guys, I got something for ya'!" called Liz as she took a couple of carrots from her pocket. Rocky ran up to her at his usual spark filled trot, but Angel didn't come up behind and push him away.

"Angel! Here girl!" Liz called again. Then she found her at the end of the paddock that was closest to the end of the driveway. She turned her head, and only when she saw Rocky munching on a carrot, did she come storming over to push Rocky off and to get her treat.

Liz was worried; Angel was always first at the gate to get a treat or to be brought inside for the night. Maybe Angel was looking for Heather. Maybe she didn't realize her finally found friend wasn't coming back this time.

Liz hoped Angel would come to accept this loss and live the life she'd now been given. Yet she had her doubts; she remembered the first time Heather and Angel had seen each other at the vet clinic, the look in her eyes and the determination to get closer to Heather. Liz felt bad for Angel. That her best, and finally found friend, had been lost so soon.

"Let's see, tomorrow I need to pick up hay and shavings so I better clean the bed of the pickup out," Liz thought out loud. Liz headed out to the barn, grabbing a broom as she went. Once she was at the pickup, she climbed on the bed and began to sweep the hay and shavings that were left over from the last trip. It took half an hour to clean it out thoroughly. But once it was done it looked brand new. She always cleaned it out so it looked that way so she knew there wasn't much of a chance that there was anything that could stick to the hay and make Rocky and Angel sick.

She set the broom in the barn, said good night, and headed toward the house. She made herself some pasta, and sat down at the table and started to eat. As she did, she began to worry about Angel. *How would Angel take in what was happening? Would she change? What would she do?* The thoughts whirled about in Liz's mind. She finished eating then headed to take a shower.

Once done with her shower, she put her pajamas on, and went and sat on her bed. She took the book *Sea Star*, which was one of her favorites and began to read. After a few chapters, she set the book down and turned out the light and started to fall asleep. But that didn't seem to happen. For a dream came, and not the best of dreams either. She stood in the paddock; Angel was standing at the other end of the paddock. Every time she reached for the mare's halter, Angel would gallop away screaming as loud as she could. Then it started to rain and the fog rolled in. Angel and her solid black coat blended right in. Soon Liz could only hear the drumming of hoof beats coming and going. "Angel! Angel!" Liz cried out, but Angel didn't respond.

Liz jolted from her bed, sweat on her forehead. She lay there for a while trying to figure out what the dream meant. The rest of the night she just lay in her bed, reading, thinking, doing anything to stay awake. The minutes seemed to drag on forever. Finally Liz gave up and went to sleep.

OOO

The next day Liz went through her routine of turning out Angel and Rocky. Then she got in the car and headed off to get hay and shavings. She drove down the road to the farm where she always got her hay. She loaded up and then unloaded it into her barn. Then she headed out to a lumberyard to get shavings. By the time everything was put away and cleaned up, she barely had time to bring in the horses and give them a grooming. Once in the house she flopped on the bed and fell to sleep, too tired to do anything else.

THE STORM

Soon, two months passed by without Heather's spirit and smile around the barn. Liz was slowly recovering, and with the help of Kurt, was able to work with Rocky and Angel. But it was hard. Each day, Angel grew farther away, and it became harder and harder to reach her.

Liz stopped sweeping the barn aisle and looked out at Angel. The mare stood there, her head pointed toward the road. She was still waiting for Heather to come back. *How can I tell her she's not going to come back?* Liz thought to herself. At that moment a car came up the road. Angel's head shot up and she gave a piercing scream. She spun around on her hind legs and went in wide circles. She screamed, bucked, reared and jumped. As the car drove past the driveway, Angel became angry and confused. She pinned her ears and set off along the paddock fence that lined the road. Galloping wildly and screaming as if telling the car to stop. As the car drove on and the fence came to an end she whirled around, screaming loudly and wildly bucking and rearing.

Liz couldn't bear to see her in this state, but there didn't seem to be anything she could do. She set her broom down and walked to the pasture gate. She clipped a lead to Rocky's halter and led him to the barn. Angel stood over in the corner of the paddock, not even bothering to turn her head. Liz walked into the paddock; she knew what would happen once she got to the mare's head. It happened every time. Angel would turn her head, teeth bared and ears pinned. Then she would either rear up at her or turn and buck, her feet just missing Liz's head.

She walked up to Angel; the mare's head was down almost touching the ground.

"Angel, easy girl. Easy," she soothed, as she got closer.

As Liz clipped the lead to the ring on the halter, it seemed to bring Angel back to life. She shot a nasty look at Liz, before rearing up in the air and striking the air with her legs. She gave an ear-piercing scream, then headed off at a gallop around the paddock.

"Easy Angel. Easy girl," Liz said as she tried to sooth the mare. But Angel was in no position to listen. She bucked wildly and violently as she flew around Liz in wide, dizzying circles.

"Come on, easy now," Liz kept saying hoping the mare would calm down. But Angel didn't, she kept galloping, screaming, bucking and rearing. Hot tears swelled up in Liz's eyes. Tears of disappointment, fear and grief. As Angel continued to gallop wildly around her, the lead rope came dangerously close to the mare's hooves.

The night clouds started to swallow up the earth and rain began to fall. It fell heavily as it spattered against Liz's face.

"Go on Angel! Go on!" Liz screamed at the top of her lungs. She ran toward the mare, flailing her arms and running.

"It wasn't my fault! Heather died! She's not coming back! It wasn't my fault!" Liz screamed as she ran after the mare flailing her arms. Angel stopped and looked at her, not sure what was going on or what to do. Yet, she didn't stop for long. Liz ran at her flailing her arms and screaming.

"It wasn't my fault! It wasn't my fault!" Liz screamed over and over. Angel wasn't sure about how to respond, she kept galloping as the wind and rain hit her face. Then thunder started to make itself heard. Liz ignored it and kept screaming and yelling, they were both in a sweat.

The rain beat down hard at both their faces, and the thunder boomed loud in their ears. As Liz ran in another giant circle chasing Angel, she tripped and fell. The ground was hard, cold, and wet on her face. She lay there and cried helplessly. She didn't know how long she sat there on the ground. Her nose was bleeding, and her short, blonde hair was plastered to her face, but she didn't care. She sat there feeling helpless and alone.

The rain continued to soak her clothes, and the thunder hurt her ears. But all she could think about was, *Have I failed? What have I done wrong?* That's all she could think about as she lay face down on the ground. Her thoughts were broken by something ruffling her hair and licking her neck. She pulled her face from the mud, only to see Angel's big dark eyes staring into hers.

"It wasn't my fault Angel," she murmured, "Heather died in a car crash. I want her back too. But she's not coming back," she looked deep into the mare's eyes and saw an understanding look in them. "If we work together, we can get through this."

They sat there for a moment looking into each other's eyes. Liz put her arm around Angel's neck and pulled herself to her feet. She looked down and saw the cotton of the lead-rope had been torn from the metal clip. She paid it no mind as she walked to the gate. As she went to close it, she saw Angel's wet, black face staring

41

at her. She took hold of the mare's halter and led her into the barn.

Inside, Rocky was quietly pulling at the hay in his hayrack. Liz led Angel to her stall and shut the door. She walked into the tack room and grabbed the water scrapper. She walked back into Angel's stall and started to make nice smooth swooping movements with the plastic stick. Water came pouring off the mare and started to form puddles on the floor. The mare stood quietly and started to eat some of the grain from her bucket.

"Good girl Angel. Good girl," Liz praised the mare. It had been a month since Angel had stood and eaten quietly. She usually always paced and snorted. That or she would turn and stand with her head in the corner and refuse to come to her bucket.

Liz got a towel and dried the mare off the best she could. That's about when she realized just how wet and cold she was herself. Her jeans and sweatshirt were soaked right to her skin. Her teeth started to chatter, but she continued to rub the wet mare down. When Angel finished her grain she started to take small bites of hay from her hayrack.

Liz finished rubbing and calming down Angel before going over to check on Rocky, who was just finishing his hay and looking for a place to lie down and sleep. He seemed fine so she went over and sat in Angel's stall as the mare ate her hay. She was exhausted, but she felt weird. Not bad, not good, but not any better than she had been. She glanced at her watch, it was 8:15pm. She knew she should go in and get some sleep, but she wanted to be sure Angel settled in after what happened in the pasture. She dozed off to sleep before she could stop herself.

UUU

Liz woke with a jolt at the feel of something on her face. She opened her eyes to see Angel. The mare's thick mane and forelock hid part of her face, but she could still see the bright, white, star. She looked at her watch again, 9:02pm. She scrambled to her feet. It was late and she was going to get sick sitting out in the barn with wet clothes on. She looked over to see both Angel's corner bucket and hayrack empty. She patted the mare then headed for the house.

A BEGINNING AND A DREAM

The next morning, Liz woke up feeling refreshed in a way. She took a long hot shower like she had the night before. Then, after getting dressed and eating a couple of muffins, Liz headed to the barn. As she walked through the door, Rocky greeted her with a cheerful whinny as always. But this morning there were two cheerful whinnies. Liz stepped back a minute and looked at the two rows of stalls. Rocky on the left, Angel on the right. Yet this time, Angel's face could be seen through the bars of the window on the stall door.

Liz looked from one stall to the other. Both horses were looking through their windows at her.

"Hey guys. How's everybody doing this morning?" Liz asked as she rubbed each horse's forehead, before putting their halters on. She led Rocky out to the paddock first. He trotted around before stopping to graze. Liz walked back to the barn and opened Angel's stall door. The mare snorted a greeting before rubbing her face against Liz's chest. She murmured to the mare before leading her out to the paddock.

Instead of going over to stand in the corner, she walked up alongside Rocky and started to graze. Liz was amazed. It had been a month since Angel had quieted down to graze. Liz turned and went back to the barn to muck stalls. She got a wheelbarrow and a shovel and set to work. After the stalls were close to immaculate, she filled the wheelbarrow with shavings and spread it out in the stalls. She felt like the weight that she'd been carrying for so long, was lifted from her shoulders.

Angel had always seemed to push Rocky away. And being that he was a herd animal that had lived in the wild part of his life, all he wanted was another horse friend to be with and play with. Rocky looked at Angel, who grazed at his side, this was a change for him. Yet he snorted and continued to graze, liking the company.

Liz smiled before heading into the house. She had to go get groceries today. She went inside and grabbed her purse and car keys before going back outside. She got into her pickup and continued to smile as both horses watched her leave.

Once her errands were done, she filled the feed buckets and the hayracks before bringing Angel and Rocky into the barn. She brought Angel in first. As she walked back out to get Rocky, she heard the gelding calling for Angel, and Angel called back. *Are they friends? Do they like or love each other or something?* Liz thought as she led a jumpy Rocky into the barn. "There you go. Eat up," Liz said as she looked at the two horses eating contently in the warm, clean stalls. She gave each of them a thorough brushing before turning out the light and going to the house.

She made some roast beef and mashed potatoes and sat at the kitchen table to eat. She sat and thought about what had happened in the past few days. She thought about the major change in Angel. *What had happened that night? What had changed Angel and I?* Liz thought about it over and over as she ate.

When she was done eating she put her pajamas on and sat on her bed and began to read. She was reading

Sea Star. No matter how many times, she always read something or understood something that she hadn't before. She was probably reading it for the 15th time. But she still found the book new, exciting and sad.

She read a couple chapters before turning out the light. That night she had another dream. This one was much different. She stood in the middle of a vast valley. She saw Heather standing at the opposite end, looking back at her. Heather's hair floated in the air, but there was no wind.

"Heather! Heather!" Liz called as she ran toward her. Just as she got to her, she disappeared into thin air.

"She's been waiting for you," said a voice behind her. She spun around to see Heather standing there in a white robe.

"What do you mean? Who?" Liz asked in confusion. But Heather disappeared again.

"She's waiting for you. She knew she was angering you," Heather appeared again, but behind Liz.

"Who's waiting for me? Who?" Liz asked again.

"She will save you, guide you, and comfort you. She will make you laugh, and she will make you cry. Listen to her!" Heather said sounding sterner.

"Who? Who?" Liz kept looking for an answer.

"Do not push her away, look down on her, or mistake her actions. She will save you, guide you, and comfort you," Heather said, disappearing and reappearing in a circle around Liz.

"Who will do these things, Heather? Who?"

"You are yet to find out my child. When the time comes you will know," Heather said before disappearing. Yet this time she did not come back.

"Heather! Heather, where did you go? Where are you?" Liz asked in alarm. Then she realized that she was no longer standing in the valley, but in amongst the clouds. She saw something coming toward her. "Heather? Is that you?" she questioned as she took a step. Then she saw it. It was a big black horse! As it came closer she realized who it was. It was Angel! "Angel!" Liz called. But the mare stopped and looked at her. The clouds started to hide her from sight. Liz saw the mare perk her ears and it was followed by a loud, cheerful whinny.

Liz's eyes flew open and she sat up in her bed. *What does this mean?* She asked herself. Liz walked to the kitchen to get a drink of water. *Angel? Angel will save, guide and comfort me, and make me laugh and cry? How will she save me? What's going to happen?* Liz thought as she drank her water. She pushed the thoughts from her mind and went back to bed.

Liz had a hard time getting back to sleep. Finally, she calmed herself down and dozed off to sleep. She did not dream any more that night.

THE ODD GAME

It was three days later, and Liz was sitting on the pasture fence writing in her journal. She did this every once in a while when she had something to write about or if she had a little free time. She sat with her back to the inside of the paddock, as she watched a couple of robins flying around chasing each other. As they landed on a branch, they puffed out their little red breasts in pride before taking off again.

Liz watched until she felt a tug at the back of her pants. She turned around to see Angel trotting off with her green cloth in her mouth.

"Angel, bring that back. Now," Liz yelled, jumping into the paddock. The mare threw her head high in the air and continued to trot around. Liz always kept the cloth in her pocket; she used it to wipe the horse's faces or her face. It had been Heather's before she died, but Liz had begun to use it after Heather's death. Angel threw it up, and it landed on the ground. Before Liz could grab it, she ran over and picked it up. After grasping it in her teeth, she threw it up again. This time it landed at Liz's feet. Liz picked it up and was about to put it in her pocket when she thought of something.

She threw it as hard as she could, and the cloth flew through the air and landed about halfway across the paddock from where they were standing. Angel gave an excited snort before trotting over and picking it up. Liz couldn't help but laugh. She looked at the mare, who stood there with her eyes and ears alert and picking up every sight and sound, but stood there with a dark green cloth hanging from her mouth. Angel, who was obviously pleased with herself, gave a snort and came over and dropped it at her feet.

Liz bent down to pick it up, when Angel took hold of the hood on her shirt and flipped it down over Liz's eyes, before cantering off. Liz stood up laughing, as she flipped the hood away from her face. Rocky stopped grazing and looked around to see what was going on. Angel's crow black coat was full of mud from when she'd rolled that morning, but she still looked beautiful as she pranced about. Her neck arched, her ears perked, her eyes bright. Angel shook her head with a snort and came over to Liz. Liz threw the cloth and Angel set off again, strutting her stuff as she went.

Liz fell back into the fence, laughing. Angel's forelock flopped back and forth as she shook her head violently, as if trying to kill the cloth. Angel threw it in the air and went chasing after it. Liz let herself out of the paddock and ran to the house to get her digital camera.

She got back to the paddock just as Angel gave the rag another good toss. Liz snapped pictures left and right. She ran around in the paddock, trying to get a good angle. Soon Rocky was piped up and in the action of chasing the rag too. Then Angel picked up the rag and brought it over and stood in front of Liz. Liz took the rag and gave it a good toss. Angel and Rocky wheeled around and set off at a fast canter. Rocky got to it first and flung it in the air.

After a couple of more throws, Liz got the cloth and walked out of the paddock and into the barn. She set the rag on the desk in her office before going inside to download the pictures to her computer. Most of her pictures were a blur or the light wasn't right. But there were a few that were good. One was of Angel and Rocky running after the rag, but you wouldn't know that's what they were doing. Another was of Angel with the rag in her mouth as she trotted around, her neck arched, looking pleased with herself. There were others of Rocky and Angel trotting around, with and without the rag in their mouths.

Liz sat there and made the pictures into a document. She typed under each one of them what was going on in the picture, and who was in the picture. It took about an hour and a half to set things right and in order. Once she was done, she went out and started to scoop the feeds. After doing the hay and the water, she walked out and brought Angel and Rocky into the barn. Once the horses were inside, Liz went and fetched a couple of brushes from the cabinet.

First she set to work on brushing the mud from Angel's coat. The mare ate contently as she pulled at the hay in her hayrack, after finishing her grain. Rocky started a conversation every once in while. All of a sudden Liz found herself telling Angel about the dream she'd had a couple days ago. Angel and Rocky listened as they ate. She asked open questions, as she went.
"She told me you'd make me laugh and cry. That you'd guide, comfort, and *save* me. I wonder what that means," Liz said as she gave a final swipe with the brush.

Liz let herself out of Angel's stall, then went in and started on Rocky. Rocky wasn't as caked with mud as Angel had been, but he had a lot of it on his face, as well as in his ears! Liz laughed as she began her new project. She gave him as thorough a brushing as she had

Angel. The gelding's eyes began to drop as he sat there and enjoyed the attention. She sat there and talked to him. Thanking him for being there, when no one else was. Rocky turned to face her as if to say, *Yes, I remember that too!*

Liz couldn't help but feel that horses could understand the human language, but just couldn't speak it. She brushed Rocky until he looked decent, but he needed a bath if she was going to get him any cleaner. As she stepped out of the stall, Rocky stuck his nose through the bars and looked at her. His eyes full of curiosity and love. *He doesn't seem to be looking at me.* Liz thought as she looked at him more closely. Liz turned around and was amazed at what she saw.

Angel was standing with her head pushed against the bars too. Liz stepped back, and the two horses gave a snort and started to carry on a conversation of the mind. Liz had never seen anything like it. *My horses are in love!* Liz thought excitedly to herself as she listened to the two, grunt, snort, whinny and pace. She knew there was more to the conversation on the mental side, but on the outside it was a pure show of love.

Liz turned off the light and left the two "love birds" to talk amongst themselves. She went inside, had a quick dinner and slipped into bed. That's when she remembered the dream again. Heather told her that Angel would make her laugh. Liz ran through the day's events and realized that's just what happened. *What's going on? What am I supposed to do?* Liz lay there in bed and thought about it, before rolling over and falling to sleep.

KURT'S HOUSE

The next morning, Liz found herself busy and scrambling. She was trying to get everything done fast so she could start training with Angel. She put the horses out in the field before doing the quickest "mucking out of the stalls" you have ever seen. Then cleaned and refilled the water buckets, before filling those in the pasture; and left the aisle to be cleaned later.

She ran to her office/tack room, and started to clean the bridle and saddle she'd gotten for Angel. The saddle soap got on her hands, jeans and shirt, as she rubbed it in with a saddle sponge. The saddle she'd bought was a Western saddle; it could be used for the trails or a show. Liz figured that was the best saddle to start out on, before moving on to a fancy western or English saddle. Along with the saddle, Liz purchased a snaffle bridle. The man at the tack store told her it was one of the more comfortable bits and was a good starting bridle. Liz hoped he was right.

Once the tack was clean, she brought Angel in from the pasture, and started to tack her up. She didn't have a problem with just sniffing at them. Her nostrils quivered as she took in the saddle's scent. Angel was fine, until Liz set the saddle on her back. The mare reared up, and it was so sudden and hard, Liz was grateful she didn't pull the cross tie ring from the wall of her stall. The mare snorted and the whites of her eyes showed the fear and annoyance.

"Easy girl. It's okay Angel. Easy girl," Liz soothed, but the mare continued to eye Liz cautiously. Liz put the saddle on the floor and walked over to calm the mare down. Just as she reached Angel, Kurt's truck pulled up. He jumped out and started walking toward the barn. Liz gave Angel a final pat before walking out of the stall to greet him.

"Long time, no see," Liz said as they started to chat. He told her how busy he and his family had been. He had three daughters and a son. His son was 17, and his daughters were, 11, 8, and 6. So Liz knew he had his hands full 24 by 7. He told her how they had just bought a house that was not too far from Liz's house. They had wanted some horses of their own, so they had purchased enough horses for the whole family to go riding together. "I have a bay, Barb mare and my wife has a brown Barb mare. My son got a chestnut, Hanoverian gelding; and my daughters had a hard time picking, but finally made a decision," he stopped to reach through the fence and scratch Rocky. "My 11 year-old has a palomino Morab gelding, my 8 year-old got a grulla, Russian Trotter mare, and my 6 year-old has a gray, Irish Hunter, a gelding also."
"Wow! That's a lot of horses. Can you handle them all okay?" Liz asked as she thought how much time and money all those horses would be.
"Yes, everybody knows that if they don't feed, groom, and exercise their horse, they lose them," he said as he started to walk toward the barn. *That's a bit harsh. But it's a good deal to have a barn full of loving faithful companions.* Liz thought to herself.
"How's Angel been?" Kurt asked hesitantly.

"She's been great. Yeh, she's much better," Liz said quite quickly. Kurt looked a little startled but nodded his head in an approving way. "I came over to see if you would like to look at our horses. The kids are dying to show them off," Kurt said sounding a bit hesitant. "We're all moved in, that's why I haven't been over here and have taken time off work. You're welcome to come now," he went on and explained.

"Sure, I'll come over now, just let me get Angel finished here," Liz said as she picked up her tack and went to put it back in the tack room/office. *Why does he seem so hesitant?* Liz asked herself as she turned of the room lights.

Once Angel was in her paddock, Liz grabbed a few carrots and got into her truck. She followed behind Kurt wondering what the horses would look like. Liz also wondered how Kurt was going to handle everything; he hadn't sounded too convincing when he'd told her. It was a fifteen-minute drive down the road. They pulled in and Liz started to look around. There was a concrete barn with about ten stalls that lined its sides. There was a small corral that seemed to be serving as an arena; for the other two paddocks were occupied with horses. As she got out of the car, Kurt's three daughters came running up and introduced themselves.

The 11-year-old was Brittany. She had dark, curly hair and brown eyes like her mom, Chris. Sarah was 8, and had blonde hair and blue eyes like Kurt. Danielle was 6 years old, and had hazel eyes and blonde hair. And Kurt's son was tall, thin and he had brown hair, but blue eyes, like a mix between his mother and father. His name was Michael. He shook her hand before walking off to the barn.

"Come on! Come see our new pretty horses!" said Danielle as she pulled on Liz's shirt.

"Danielle, don't rush," Kurt said sternly.

"It's okay," Liz said, trying not to sound surprised. The girls led Liz to the barn as Kurt and Chris walked behind her. Danielle walked up to the paddock and whistled. All the horse's ears pricked up and they came trotting over to the fence.

"This is Star," said Danielle patting a gray gelding's neck, "he's an Irish Hunter."

"Sonny's a Morab," said Brittany as she walked up to her palomino gelding.

"Misty here is a Russian Trotter. Don't you think she has a neat color?" Brittany said quickly, as she offered her horse a carrot piece. The horse was a blue roan, a very odd color.

"Yes, they're all beautiful," said Liz as she tried to keep up with the children's fast talking manner.

"Liz, could I show you something?" Kurt said as he walked up behind her. Liz followed him into the barn and to a stall. Liz looked in.

"I don't see anything," Liz looked into the stall, letting her eyes adjust to the darkness. Kurt picked up a lead rope and went into the stall. He led out a small bay pony, only about 13 hands high.

"Who's this?" questioned Liz as she looked at the horse's matted mane and tail.

"This is Bean. He's a Pindos pony that our clinic rescued," Kurt said as he tried to comb the pony's mane with his fingers. Bean jumped at the touch of Kurt's hand.

"Easy now, easy," soothed Kurt as he patted Bean's neck.

"I volunteered to keep him. But that was before we started getting the other horses. We're having trouble with him because he doesn't get much attention," Kurt stopped to soothe the gelding again.

"He's 9-years-old, and was gelded at the clinic. We were wondering if you had the time and space for another horse."

Liz agreed that she'd take the pony, and went home to get her trailer. She went quickly and made a stall ready with thick bedding before heading back to Kurt's house. The pony was very jumpy and nervous, and Liz hoped she'd made the right choice. She brought the gelding home and wondered what was really going on with Kurt and his family.

THE NEW ONES

Liz pulled into her driveway, and Bean immediately started calling. Angel and Rocky came cantering to the fence and called back. Liz stopped the car, jumped out and opened the trailer door. After lowering the ramp, she opened up the door that was on Bean's side. As soon as the door was open, Bean's hind feet came flying out. They just missed Liz's face as she ducked.

"There'll be none of that, Bean!" Liz hollered into the trailer. She led the gelding out and over to his stall.

He began to pace and scream for the others, who he knew were out in the pasture. Angel and Rocky began to pace around the pasture gate.

"All right. You can come in," Liz replied as she walked out to the gate. She picked up the lead-ropes that she kept by the gate and led them in, one in each hand. This was the first time she'd done this, and the two horses walked calmly on either side of her. She put Rocky in his stall, and then put Angel in hers.

The barn was full of calling, screaming, pawing, and pacing. Liz quickly scooped the feeds into their carrying buckets, but didn't give it out. Liz went into her office and called Kurt.

"Hello, vet Kurt Lutgens," he answered.

"Kurt, it's Liz. I was wondering what and how much feed Bean's on," Liz asked.

"Oh, well, he just got hay here. So you might have to devise a feeding schedule on your own," Kurt replied hesitantly.

"Kurt, are you all right? Is everything okay?" Liz asked in a worried voice.

"No. We're having a lot of financial difficulties. We've been at this house for a year. I haven't been over to see you because of what's happening," he poured out the story.

"Oh, I'm sorry. Do you need any help?"

"No, we're moving, out of the state. Horses n' all! That's why we needed to find Bean a home," he answered, sounding guilty.

"Well, when are you leaving?" Liz questioned, feeling sorry for them.

"Next month. We'll be busy 'til then so we probably won't see much of you."

"Give a call if you need anything," Liz tried to comfort Kurt.

"Will do. Bye," and with that he hung up.

Liz returned to the aisle to find the horses still carrying on a conversation. She picked up a brush and went into Bean's stall.

"Easy boy," she soothed as she neared him. He eyed her cautiously. *I want to help, but did I make the right choice in bringing this gelding to my house?* Liz thought as she carefully combed the snargles from Bean's mane. Once his mane was done, Liz started on his tail. As she reached for it, Bean's hind feet came swinging outward from underneath him, coming dangerously close to Liz's head and skimming her shin.

"Hey! Easy! There will be no kicking in this barn!" Liz scolded. The gelding threw his head in the air and squealed. She reached for his tail again, this time the little horse jumped backward. Liz was about to scold him again, when she looked at his eyes. He rolled the whites of them, and his nostrils flared. Liz remembered, and had to remember that Bean was a rescue horse, and probably abused before he was found. She talked to and soothed Bean, and decided that was enough adventure for one day. She stood back and looked at him.

"You could put on a little weight," she said running her hand along Bean's side and feeling his ribs. She walked back to the feed room and scooped out what she thought was a reasonable amount of feed for Bean.

She picked up the three feed buckets and headed down the aisle, pouring the grain into the buckets one by one. Bean eyed the feed as if he'd never seen it before, and he probably hadn't. Liz scooped some up into her hand and offered it to the horse. He sniffed it and after looking it over, he took a little bite. Then he took another. Liz finally dropped the little she had left into his bucket and he ate it from there. After getting everybody hay she turned out the barn lights and headed inside to get some sleep.

∪∪∪

The next two days, Liz went through her regular barn routine. As Bean became comfortable, Liz thought he needed a new name. The day came when Liz thought it was time that he went out to pasture with Angel and

Rocky instead of being walked around in the arena or yard.

Liz clipped a lead rope to Bean's halter and led him outside. She didn't want to rename him until she saw him in action. She led him to the gate, and he stood quietly while she unhooked the chain. Angel and Rocky stood side-by-side and watched from a distance as she walked him into the pasture, unhooked the lead, and slipped back out. Bean gave a high-pitched squeal before turning on his haunches and taking off at a gallop around the pasture. He stopped only for a moment as he felt fresh, summer grass beneath his hooves. The other two soon joined in on the fun and were one herd as they galloped around talking to each other as they went.

Once they came to a stop, they started to check each other out. They sniffed each other and went muzzle to muzzle. Angel established her place at the top, but Rocky just wanted a friend, Bean seemed the same way, so they didn't care. They stopped, and started to graze. That's when Liz noticed a dog sitting at the far corner of the pasture. Liz clapped her hands and whistled, the dog came right up to her. It was a male, German Shepard puppy. It couldn't have been more than two months old. He had a ripped up collar around his neck with a cardboard tag that said BOSCO.

She ran her hand along his side and felt his ribs. She took his collar off, and went into the house. She picked up the phone and dialed the town animal shelter.

"Hello, Walt's Animal Shelter. How may I help you?" answered a man's voice on the other end.

"Hi, I have a stray German Shepard puppy here. He has a tag that says, Bosco on it. I'm not sure what to do with the dog," Liz explained as she fiddled with the collar.

"Well, we haven't had a report of any missing dogs. What shape is the dog in?"

"It looks like he's been lost for a while, and he only looks like he's about two months old," Liz explained further.

"Well you can bring him here, but we're full so he'll be put to sleep tomorrow if no one picks him up. Or you can keep him, your choice," and with that he hung up.

Liz sat there in awe for a moment. *How can they be so careless of an animal's well being?* Liz asked herself as she went back outside.

The dog was still sitting in the same place. He looked at her curiously as she walked toward him.

"Bosco, come here boy," Liz called as she came to a stop. The dog eagerly trotted up.

"Well, you're staying here. You're part of the family now. I'll never let them take you," she said as the dog started to give her slobbery kisses.

LEARNING TOGETHER

The next day, Liz walked into the barn; she was greeted by three cheerful whinnies. She went to each one and gave them a carrot. Bean was looking much more cheerful then he had been. Liz had been thinking of a new name for him, but decided she needed to see him out with the others some more. She didn't bother giving them feed. It was the middle of summer, and the grass was green and lush, so Liz didn't see a need to feed them grain or hay in the morning.

She led Rocky out first, being that he stood quietly and allowed for his halter to be put on, when the others didn't. She unclipped the lead at the gate, and the Mustang started calling for his pasture mates. As she went back to Angel's stall, the mare let her slip the halter over her head and lead her out. Finally she came back to Bean's stall. He stood there, impatiently waiting to go out.

At first, he would have no part of the halter. But he soon realized that he couldn't go out with his newfound friends until he allowed it on. Liz led him outside, but stopped herself a few feet from the gate and thought, *Okay I'll let them out for a while, then I'll work on Angel.* She made her plan and put Bean in the pasture. He was a daring little pony, who didn't seem to know how small he was compared to 15 hand Rocky and 15.3 hand Angel. He went right up and gave Angel a nip on the butt before tearing off across the paddock, with Angel flying at his heels.

The little guy was a small 13.1 hand pony with the heart and courage of a 17-hand horse. Liz thought he should have a big brave sounding name. *But what should it be?* She thought and thought, as she leaned on the paddock fence and watched as the little gelding nipped Rocky and they repeated the act over again.

A high-pitched whine broke Liz's thoughts. She remembered then, *Bosco!* Liz ran to the barn. She'd put the puppy in the tack room for the night with some leftover turkey from dinner. She had to "puppy proof" her house, which she'd done, immediately, last night. She put him in there because she usually went in there first every morning. She opened the tack room door and a little brown and black figure came flying out and down the hall. She ran to catch up with him; worried that being locked in there had scared him.

She found the little puppy running around the horses, barking wildly. The horses watched yet didn't seem phased by the puppy's appearance. She sighed a breath of relief and went to get started on the stalls.

"That's it!" hollered Liz as she ran to the pasture, "Captain! Captain instead of Bean!" Liz had been thinking the whole time as she cleaned the stalls. The names that might have worked, like Chance, hadn't fit his personality. *But Captain just might do it!* She thought as she went to the pasture fence. She called Bean, knowing he would come to that one. He walked up and stood still as she thought about it.

"What about Captain?" she whispered to the gelding. He looked at her and snorted as if trying to answer.

"Captain! Captain it is!" Liz said in a proud tone.

She realized then that if she didn't start training with Angel, she wouldn't fit it in today. She called the mare to the gate and brought her to her stall. Liz got the tack and walked into the stall with it. The mare sniffed it curiously before allowing it to be put on her. She was a bit tense, but with a little encouragement, allowed both the saddle and bridle to come on and off without a problem.

Liz left the tack on as she walked the mare out to her little arena she'd built. She led the mare around to get her used to the tack before bringing her up to the mounting block. Angel seemed fine as she sat there next to the mounting block. Liz swung her leg over the mare's back, and Angel became extremely tense. Liz got her feet in the stirrups and let the mare sit there, just letting her know that she didn't have to do anything until she was ready. Finally, when Angel seemed relaxed, Liz asked her to go forward. The mare moved forward stiffly and hesitantly. They made a few laps around the ring as both horse and rider started to relax.

Liz felt the powerful, long, smooth strides of the big, Friesian mare beneath her. Angel moved like a dream, even at a walk. Liz calmly asked the mare to trot, and Angel did so. They glided around the ring at an even trot. Liz found her seat and began to post. The mare had a wonderful stride and gait. Liz started laughing, as she remembered how she'd bought this wonderful mare for $55. *What blind fools!* Liz thought to herself as Angel began to relax.

When Liz thought that Angel had had enough, she dismounted and led her to the barn. She gave the mare the longest, most thorough rubdown she'd ever had. She gave Angel an apple before bringing the two geldings in and giving everyone their dinner. Bosco jogged along beside her as they made their way around with grain, hay, and water. Bosco seemed to love jumping for the dirty water that she tossed from the buckets. He also liked eating the grain that fell from the horses' mouths to the floor.

Liz laughed at the funny things this dog did and was glad to have him around to cheer the place up a bit. She turned out the barn lights after brushing everybody, and headed toward the house. Liz still couldn't get Captain to let her groom out his tail, or brush his hindquarters. She guessed he'd been hit or beat back there and wanted to know why. She was making good progress with Rocky, who seemed to have had a bad experience with the saddle and bridle.

Liz suddenly noticed that she was helping a bunch of horses that needed help, time, and TLC. She went into the house and poured Bosco a bowl of food she'd bought last night, before getting herself a bowl of soup. She sat in the living room, watching ANIMAL PLANET, while Bosco lay at her feet. She finished her dinner and went to bed, waiting for the next day to come.

∪∪∪

"Easy girl, canter," commanded Liz as she and Angel trotted around the ring. It was two days later and Angel was making big improvements. The mare broke into an easy, yet, tense canter. Liz soothed her and brought her back to a trot, until she was ready.
"Canter," Liz said again once Angel relaxed a bit. This time the mare broke into an easy canter, and they flew

around the arena, Angel's powerful strides eating up the ground beneath them. She then seemed to go faster and faster.

After a few circuits, Liz brought the mare to a halt and led her to the barn. Once dismounting, Liz couldn't wait to see how the mare would do on the trails tomorrow. But for now she had to go get hay and shavings.

TRUST ME

The next day Liz was busy getting Rocky used to the saddle, when she heard Bosco barking hysterically. She dropped the tack she was holding outside of Rocky's stall, and ran outside. Only to find the puppy running around Angel and Captain, barking as loud as he could. The two horses just watched the little dog, but didn't seem at all scared or startled. They stood there and acted like the dog had always been there, traveling with them.

Liz smiled before returning to Rocky's stall. She picked up the tack and entered the stall. The Mustang retreated to the far corner and showed the whites of his eyes. Liz soothed him before placing the saddle on his back. Rocky tensed and stepped away, but Liz was able to get him to stand so she could tighten the girth. Rocky stood there and with her calm voice, Liz settled him down enough so she could slip the bridle over his head. He shook his head violently as she tightened the last strap, but didn't move away.

Liz led him outside to the arena. It was now the beginning of autumn and the warm autumn breezes drifted through the air. It would be Rocky's first time with a rider on his back. Liz walked him around like she always did, before halting him next to the mounting block. *He's a Wild Mustang, so be careful.* Liz reminded herself as she gathered her reins. She swung lightly into the saddle, and the horse beneath her immediately tensed up.

"It's okay. Easy boy, easy," Liz soothed as they sat there. Liz didn't ask the horse to do anything until he was ready. It might take longer, but she thought it was only fair to the animal.

Rocky began to relax, and she asked him to move forward. He tensed, but started to walk. His stride was short and choppy as they made their way around the ring. Liz felt the horse start to relax and she praised him in a calm voice,

"Good boy, Rocky. Good boy." They walked around the ring a dozen times before Liz halted him, and dismounted.

She walked him back to the barn and gave him a good long rubdown until his coat shone with elegance. Liz had finished training with Angel and had started working Rocky the week before. He was making progress ever so slowly. Always needing to know you were there. She gave him some hay before heading out to the pasture gate to get the others.

"Angel! Captain!" Liz called as she opened the gate. The two horses came trotting up to Liz. Their eyes bright with excitement. She clipped the lead onto Angel's halter and led her from the pasture. The Friesian mare danced excitedly, knowing there would be grain in the barn waiting for her. The mare's thick, black mane hung over the right side of her neck, and floated up in the breeze. Liz smiled as she led the mare into her stall. Liz headed back to the pasture for Captain. It was then that it struck her; *Kurt is now out of state. He didn't even say good-bye.* She quickly led Captain to the barn and went into the house.

Liz picked up the phone and dialed Kurt's house number. Their phone was disconnected. *I don't even know where they've gone!* Liz thought as she sat down at the kitchen table and fiddled with a pen. Kurt had been a good friend, and a very helpful vet. If it hadn't been for him, Angel and Heather would never have seen each other again. A tear rolled down Liz's cheek, and she jumped up and ran out to the barn. Bosco jumped around her feet in confusion as she went.

She ran down the barn aisle and into Angel's stall. Liz wrapped her arms around the mare's thick glossy neck and sobbed.

"He's gone! He didn't even say good-bye! I didn't get to say thank you!" Liz sobbed into Angel's warm neck. The mare turned her head slightly to see what was wrong with her friend. Liz calmed herself down and sat in the stall, rubbing Angel's black Friesian body and telling her how Kurt and she had met and helped each other. Liz felt guilty that she should have told him thank you long before this. She hadn't really realized that he would be leaving.

Liz played with strands of Angel's long, thick, black mane as she talked. All of a sudden she stopped. Liz remembered her dream. More and more of it was coming true. *She's here to comfort me, like Heather said.* Liz thought about it for a minute. *She's supposed to guide, save, and comfort me. As well as make me laugh and cry. Well, that's two down, and three to go.* Liz started to brush the horses to take her mind off never seeing Kurt again. She brushed Angel's and Rocky's coat until they shimmered with beauty.

Then Liz came to Captain's stall. The Pindos pony sat there, joyfully munching his hay. Liz let herself in and started to brush the mud and dirt from his mane. He sat there and paid no attention to what she was doing;

only knowing that it felt good. But as Liz stopped brushing his shoulder and went to his rump, the pony shot backward and rolled the whites of his eyes.

"Easy now, it's okay," soothed Liz stroking his neck. She brushed his shoulder and then slowly worked her way back again. Before either Captain or Liz new what was going on, Liz was brushing the dirt and mud off Captain's rump. Liz stopped to wipe her hands before starting to brush again.

Captain seemed to suddenly realize what Liz was doing and turned around to look at her with nervous eyes. "It's okay. You're fine, just relax, Captain," Liz said as she looked back at him. He seemed to relax a little, so Liz continued to brush his mud covered coat. Liz praised him as he stood still and let her rub down his hind legs, pick them up to clean them, and stood nice and calm as she brushed both sides of his hind-quarters. She continued to feed the pony the carrots from her pockets until they were all gone. Then started to just use words, and not treats.

The pony sat there, listening and watching her as she took all the mud from his coat and swept him clean. "I think I need to give you all a bath tomorrow," Liz said as she left Captain's stall. She looked at their dirty coats, but knew they all just needed a bath. Especially before it gets colder and windier. She went inside and sat down and ate supper before going to her room to read.

Liz read for about an hour, before she realized her bedside clock had struck 9:15pm. She set her book down and turned out the light, and fell fast asleep.

BOSCO'S TURN

"Now everybody try to stay clean," said Liz as she finished and put Angel in her stall. The mare was now sparkly and cleaner than ever. Everybody in the barn was. She looked at her three horses, who were looking through their windows. *Why didn't we go out today?* They seemed to ask. Liz laughed before handing out the evening feeds. She scooped out the feeds, adding a little more to each bucket, now that there was no more grass in the pasture.

She walked down the aisle, pushing by a frisky and sometimes annoying Bosco. She worked around him, as he scampered up and down the barn aisle, as if it were his job to patrol it. The German Shepard came and rubbed up against her leg, and gave an agitated whine. She realized that she hadn't really been paying attention to the new puppy. Liz quickly finished feeds and went into the house, Bosco following her the whole way.

Liz grabbed her purse and headed out to her car. She cleared a spot in the back seat and looked around for the dog.

"Bosco! Here boy!" she hollered. The dog came to her willingly and Liz bent down to pet his face.

"All right, up you go," Liz said as she wrapped her arms around the small puppy and lifted him into the car. She jumped into the driver's seat and started the car. Bosco sat there, his head hanging beside hers as he panted and licked Liz's face. Liz tried to concentrate on the road, but before she knew what was happening, Bosco was sitting in the passenger seat looking over at her. Liz reached over and patted the puppy's head.

Liz came to a stop in front of PET SMART, and both human and dog jumped out of the car. She had only a cotton lead rope to serve as both a collar and a leash. Liz shrugged and led Bosco into the building. The puppy started to bark and bolt at every little thing. Liz kept hold of him and led him to the "doggy" section of the store. Liz walked Bosco up and down the aisle until he calmed down enough to sit still. Liz had taught him to sit and lie down, but the puppy didn't know "stay". Liz finally got him to sit still, and looked around at the collars and leashes, knowing she needed to get at least these things on her trip.

Liz found a flashy, green collar, (the same color as the horses' halters); she found a matching green leash and walked up to one of the storekeepers.

"Excuse me, could I try this collar on my dog?" Liz asked politely. The woman turned around, she had light brown hair and dark eyes.

"Sure. Come with me," she said with a hand motion. Liz followed her to a room in the front. The woman motioned her in. The room had a metal table and windows that looked out over the parking lot. Bosco sniffed around curiously as Liz was led to the table.

"What's your dog's name?" the woman asked as she bent down to pet Bosco.

"His name's Bosco. I found him as a stray two weeks ago," Liz explained.

"Oh. Poor thing," the woman said as Bosco licked her face, "Well, let's get him on the table. Do you want a custom made tag, or what?" the woman asked as she wrapped her arms around Bosco. Liz helped her get the excited dog onto the table.

"I don't know. How much does it cost for that," Liz asked a bit hesitantly.

"Well, it depends on what shape you want, but they're about $12 a piece," she answered as she looked the dog over.

"I only need to know if this collar fits before I buy it," Liz said as she watched the woman look her dog over.

"Oh, okay," the woman said a little taken back, "Where's the collar you want?" she questioned as she looked at Liz. Liz handed her the collar and the woman looked it over and held it up to Bosco's neck before saying anything. "This will definitely fit him. It's one of our better brands of collars. It's a good, strong collar," she explained, still sounding hesitant.

"Oh, that's great. I really need that because we live on a horse farm," Liz explained, as the woman put the collar and leash in a bag.

"Could I see the tags?" Liz asked trying to sound cheerful and happy.

"Sure," the woman said as she took a display from the cabinet. It was covered in blank tags and tags that showed all of the different fonts. One of the shapes and fonts caught Liz's eye. It was a green clover, the same shade as the collar she'd bought. The font she looked at was an uppercase, block letter font.

"Could I have this tag with this font?" Liz said pointing toward the two she wanted.

"Sure it will take about fifteen minutes to make it. We just need you to fill this out so we know what you want," she explained as she handed Liz a small slip of paper.

Liz filled out the paper with the following:

NAME (PRINT) : *Mary Elizabeth Parker (Liz)*
DOG NAME : *Bosco*
TAG SHAPE: *Clover*
FONT : *Arial Black*

After filling out the slip, Liz handed it to the woman and went back to the "doggy" section of the store. She looked around now for toys and treats. She took samples of the treats and let Bosco try them. She finally figured out that he liked the vegetable ones, since he kept pulling for the bucket. *That's weird. I never knew a dog that liked veggies.* Thought Liz as she picked up a box of the one-inch, puppy size treats and put it in her cart. She also picked up a soccer ball and a tug-o-war rope before going back to the front desk to get the tag that she had ordered.

Liz paid for her purchases, and headed out to the car, with a happy looking puppy trotting by her side. She put her bags in the car and helped Bosco in before getting in herself and starting the car. Once she was on the road, Bosco jumped into the front seat like he had before and watched as the cars zoomed past his window as they went down the highway. Liz looked at Bosco, only to see Bosco looking back at her.

"You are one of a kind Bosco. You really are," Liz said as she reached over to pet him. As if he knew what she'd said, Bosco gave a big bark and wagged his tail, as if to say, *You bet I am!*

Liz laughed and sang along with the radio, until she pulled into the driveway. Bosco jumped out of the car and ran around to the back, where Liz had put his new toys, treats, collar and leash set. Liz brought the stuff inside and sat in the living room, putting the collar and tag on Bosco.

"There you go, Bosco," Liz said as she buckled the collar, (that now had the tag on it), to Bosco's neck.

Liz had a quick dinner, and went to bed, with Bosco sleeping by her bedside the whole night.

THE ICE

"Happy Thanksgiving everybody!" Liz greeted, as she walked into the barn. "Everybody's going to get a little extra something, along with their feed today," she exclaimed as she walked cheerfully into the feed corner. "Yes, you too Bosco," Liz informed as the puppy jumped around her feet. His dark, curious eyes looking up at her as she went to the grain cans. Liz scooped out the sweet feed into the pouring/carrying buckets, before heading to get the surprise. She took a five-gallon bucket from her car and went back to the feed corner to open it.

She popped the lid off and found what she was going to give them. It was a bucket full of corn. She took her scoop and added the corn to each bucket. When she was done, she picked the buckets up and headed down the aisle to hand it out. The horses ate it up greedily, and Liz thought it would be a good time to brush them while they were all standing still. Liz picked up a few brushes from the tack room and started to get to work.

Two hours later, Liz walked out of Angel's stall and looked at her now, spotless horses. Liz looked at Angel, the mare's thick, black, Friesian body, stood squared up as she looked through her barred windows. Liz went over and rubbed the mare's forehead, before walking over and taking the ball from Bosco's mouth. Liz threw it into the air, and Bosco went racing after it. Then, Liz heard a loud whinny from behind her. Liz turned around and saw Angel pawing at her stall wall. That's when Liz had an idea.

She walked into the barn and slipped the halter over Angel's head, and led her out to the pasture. Liz let her go in the pasture, and realized it wasn't fair to keep the other two inside. Liz walked to the barn and let the other two out, before trying her idea. She took the soccer ball from Bosco and threw it into the pasture. The German Shepard pup happily ran to get it. Angel saw it and ran to get it as well. She got to it, but didn't pick it up. Instead, she pushed it around in the three inches of snow that was on the ground.

Bosco got hold of it, brought it back to Liz, and ran into the pasture, waiting for it to be thrown again. Liz gave it another hard throw. This time Bosco and all the horses ran after it. They all pushed to get to it. Then it was all a disaster.

Angel lost her footing as she pushed to get the ball. She almost recovered, when she hit a spot of ice. She slid across it as she came to a stop, and lay on her side. Blood oozed from her shoulder that she'd fallen on. Liz nearly screamed as she looked at the mare, her black coat drenched with sweat. But Liz knew it would only scare the mare. She ran into the pasture, pushing Rocky and Captain away as they checked out the scene. She pushed Bosco away as well who wanted someone to throw his ball.

Angel quivered with fear and pain. Liz looked the mare over, and decided the best thing she could do was call the vet. She threw Rocky and Captain in their stalls and ran to the barn office. She dialed the town clinic and waited for someone to answer.

"Hello, Pioneer Clinic. How may I help you?" answered a man's voice on the other line.

"Hello. I have a mare who just fell on the ice and she's breathing hard, and is bleeding pretty bad," Liz explained in a worried voice. After giving the man her address, he told her what to do until he got there.

"Cover her up, keep her warm. Try to see if she'll drink any water, but make sure the water's warm. I'll be there in about twenty minutes."

Liz ran to her trunk and pulled out two big horse blankets, before running out to Angel who was still lying on her side in the paddock. The mare was still breathing heavily, and bleeding.

"Easy girl, you're gonna' be fine," Liz soothed, though she was convincing herself just as much as she was convincing Angel. She laid the blankets over Angel, tucking them under her the best she could. It seemed like ages before the vet finally arrived.

"Okay, we'll need to get her to the barn where she'll be out of the wind, snow and cold. Here we go," the man said as he took hold of Angel's tail, and Liz took hold of the mare's halter. Angel staggered to her feet and stumbled to the barn, with Liz and the vet at her side. Angel stumbled about, counting on her human friends for help.

They finally got the mare to her stall, and got her to lie down. Liz brought Angel a bucket of warm water, and she drank it up. She refilled it for the vet who was ready to start working on Angel.

"Now, what's your name," Liz asked, for they'd had no time to talk before.

"Oh. I'm Conrad Whitfield," he answered as he put his gloves on. Liz turned the lights of the stall on, and asked if there was anything she could do to help.

"Nope, I have it under control. I just sedated her so she should be okay," he answered, looking at the mare that lay in the shavings of her stall.

"It might be better if you leave. Not to be rude, but it might help her if she didn't have to concentrate on two people at once," he said as he took out a needle and a stitching thread to stitch the mare's bleeding shoulder. Liz nodded her head and walked up to the house.

She sat at the kitchen table and drank a cup of coffee, as calmly as she could. Finally, she couldn't contain her feelings any longer. She burst into tears and held her head in her hands. *The dream's coming true! Heather was right.* Liz thought as she sat there. *She's making me cry like Heather said.* Liz sat there and continued to cry, when she heard a whine. She looked over and saw Bosco sitting at her feet looking up at her with his usual curious eyes. Liz picked the puppy up and set him on her lap. Bosco started to lick her face, as if trying to cheer her up. She kissed the dog before setting him back on the floor.

But, how is Angel going to save and guide me? Well, I guess she's already guiding me. Giving me something to look forward to every day. Liz thought as she sat there with Bosco looking up at her. She bent down and stroked his face, his eyes looking at Liz's face. "It'll be okay. Angel will be fine," Liz said forcing a smile as she continued to pat the dog.

There was a knock on the kitchen door, and Liz scrambled to her feet to get it. She opened it up to find Conrad standing there. His brown, winter jacket lay unbuttoned. *It was probably warm in the barn.* Liz thought, knowing the air outside was too cold to wear an unbuttoned jacket.

"The mare's all stitched up if you want to see her," he said pointing toward the barn. Liz grabbed her coat and followed Conrad to the barn. She walked down the barn aisle, Rocky and Captain pawed at their stall doors in confusion.

"She's tired now, but she'll be perkier tomorrow," said Conrad as he looked at Liz's worried face. Angel was lying on her side, her eyes were half closed. Conrad had shaved away Angel's winter coat where he'd had to stitch her up.

"Once her hair grows back on that shoulder, you won't be able to notice it," Conrad continued to explain, "I gave her some antibiotics, but I need you to put this on the stitches, and this in her feed," he said handing her what looked like a toothpaste tube, and a small container filled with a white bran looking powder.

"Okay," Liz said as she took the stuff from his hands.

"I'll be back in about 2 to 3 weeks, if it looks good, I'll take the stitches out, if not, I'll leave them there, and see what we can do about it. All right?" he explained.

"Yep. Now should I keep her in the barn?" Liz asked.

"Certainly. You can let her out after I take the stitches out," answered Conrad.

They said goodbye, and Conrad left. *At least it wasn't as bad as it could get.* Liz thought to herself as she put the medicines in the tack room.

BIRTHDAY SURPRISE

The time came for Angel to have her stitches out. The mare had been improving with the help of the medicine Conrad said she was to have. Now Conrad said that she'd healed up nicely, and they could be taken out now.

"Easy girl, whoa now," Conrad said as he let go of her after working carefully to take them out.

"There you go Angel. Thanks Conrad," Liz said as she let go of the mare's halter and turned to Conrad.

"No problem. You just need to put this cream on her until it's empty," said Conrad as he handed Liz another toothpaste like tube.

"Okay. She can go out now right?" Liz questioned as she and Conrad walked to the feed corner to so Liz could put the cream away.

"I don't know. She might rip her cut open. I would keep her in, and just walk her around for at least five days," Conrad informed.

"Okay, I'll do that. Thanks for everything Conrad," Liz said as they walked out to the vet's truck.

Liz turned around and walked back to Angel's stall, after waving Conrad off, and looked in through the barred windows. She slipped the halter on over the mare's wide, black head, and led her outside. She walked the mare around in the foot of snow, Angel's body quivered with excitement; she hadn't been outside in three weeks. Liz walked Angel around for about 20 minutes before bringing her in along with the others. Rocky and Captain checked out the aisle for they could smell the scent of the strange vet.

Liz quickly fed them, as Bosco ran around the barn pushing his ball with his nose, and having a grand old time. Liz laughed as the pup once again jumped for the dirty water she was throwing from a bucket. She got everyone fed and watered before getting the tube of medicine Conrad had given her. She walked into Angel's stall, and the mare turned to face her. Her forelock pushed to one side, revealing her big white star. Liz smiled and stroked the mare before rubbing the soapy looking gel from the tube onto the Friesian's shoulder.

After making sure everyone was clean, Liz headed into the house. She checked her calendar that hung on the kitchen wall. "Tomorrow's January 24th," Liz murmured as she scanned the page, "Tomorrow's my birthday Bosco. I'll be another year older unfortunately." She went to the stove and made herself a bowl of chicken soup before sitting in front of the TV and watching the news. *I don't think anybody knows, but I'll turn 35 whether anyone's here or not.* Liz thought as she ate her soup. She finished eating, put food in Bosco's dish and went to bed.

∪∪∪

Liz slept in late the next morning, thinking that it was only fair for being another year older. She made herself bacon and eggs and gave the extras to Bosco who enjoyed them very much. She ate slowly and told Bosco how glad she was to have such a wonderful family of animals. Liz finished her breakfast and was washing the dishes when she heard a knock on the door. She dried her hands before going over to open it. *Conrad didn't say he was coming again. And I haven't called the dentist or the farrier. Who could it be?* Liz thought as she turned the door handle.

She opened the door to see a young woman standing outside. She was probably in her twenties; she had light brown hair, and blue eyes. She stood about the same height as Liz, around five and a half feet.

"Hello. Are you Mary Parker?" she asked in a hesitant voice. Liz wasn't used to being called Mary, but she did answer.

"Yes, I'm Liz. Who are you," Liz asked kind of quickly.

"I'm Heather's cousin, Amanda Bolton," she explained. Liz stood there in awe. She invited the woman in and offered her coffee.

"I'm sorry to drop by so unexpectedly, but I live right down the road from here. And Heather told me all about you at our Grandma's party," Amanda explained, sounding a bit hesitant.

"Oh, she seems to have told everyone," Liz said sitting back in her chair.

"I was wondering if I could see your horses. I don't mean to be nosey, but Heather described them to us and they sounded so beautiful. She said that you had her beloved Angel foal and a mustang named Rocky," the woman kept talking.

"Sure, I don't mind. C'mon," Liz said getting up to get her coat.

They walked outside as Amanda continued to talk. "I work as an exercise rider and an instructor for younger kids at a farm half an hour north of hear called Willow Brook Farm. They have all different breeds of horses."

"Wow, that sounds nice," Liz said as she opened the barn door.

"This is a nice tidy place you have here. Willow Brook is so big you can easily get lost, but this is really nice," Amanda commented as they walked into the barn.

"This is Angel, that's Rocky, and that's Captain," Liz said, pointing to each horse as she said it.

"Oh. This mare's beautiful. What's her name?" asked Amanda.

"Angel," said Liz sounding a little confused.

"No, I mean her full name," Amanda said again.

"Oh, I really never had a longer name for any of them here," Liz said a little confused by the thought and question.

"Oh, okay," Amanda said before turning to the gelding on the other side of the hallway, "You are a couple of handsome boys. Yes you are. Who's who?" she asked looking at the two horses.

"This is Rocky, he's the Mustang. And this is Captain, a horse I got from a vet who had to move. He's a Pindos pony," explained Liz. Amanda seemed more interested in Rocky and Captain than she did Angel. Liz shrugged her shoulders and scratched Angel's forehead. Amanda finished pampering the two geldings and turned to Liz.

"Angel's a Friesian, right?" Amanda asked walking over to the mare.

"Yep," Liz answered. Before Liz could tell Amanda, the woman lifted up the Friesian's forelock and saw her star.

"But she has a star! Friesian's don't have, or aren't supposed to have any white on them," Amanda was nearly yelling. Liz was taken off guard, but responded.

"I know. I bought her from an auction. She was being sold to the meat house and I had to do something. The reason she was being sold was because of her white star. Didn't Heather tell you that?" Liz explained and asked.

"No. She said you bought Angel from her father, Jake, but she didn't say why you bought him or why her father was selling her," Amanda said as she walked back across the hall to Rocky and Captain.

"Well, it's getting cold, why don't we go inside," Liz said feeling the January winds from outside blow against her back.

"Have you fed them yet this morning?" Amanda questioned as they headed for the door.

"No. But I don't want to keep you waiting."

"Oh don't worry about me I'm fine. I'll stay out of your way," Amanda insisted. Liz shrugged her shoulders and fed the horses while Amanda picked up a brush and started to groom the two geldings.

ALL NEW

"You probably should pick a barn name. I mean, what if you start showing?" Amanda questioned again as they sat at the kitchen table drinking coffee. It had been a week and a half and they had been helping each other out at the barn. Liz and Amanda had become very good friends the day Amanda had come to visit. Having both known Heather really well, they felt more like friends in a way. It had just seemed natural for the two to start helping each other, but Amanda kept asking Liz what her barn name is, or is going to be.

"I don't know. I thought about it last night, but I don't know a good name. I wouldn't want to pick a dumb one," Liz explained as they sat there flipping through magazines that they both had. Liz had gotten them out and Amanda had brought some from her house. They were looking for ideas.

"Oh, well start with a color. A color that you like and that your blankets, halters and everything else will be," Amanda explained in her fast talking manner.

"Well, I like green," Liz answered.

"That's a good color. You probably won't want to use red. Almost everybody uses red, including my stable, their colors are red and brown," Amanda kept talking as she flipped through the pages of the magazine.

"Speaking of which, do you want to come to a horse show with me? It's in two weeks. I'm the person who goes everywhere with the kids," Amanda questioned, looking up from the magazine, "it's a two hour drive South, and I'm not sure if enough folks at the barn will have time to come with me."

"Sure, but we're trying to figure out a barn name right now," Liz reminded as she looked at the slim woman. They sat there in thought for a moment, when Liz had an idea.

"What about Maple Wood? We're surrounded by maples, it would…, no, it still doesn't seem right," Liz frowned. She sat in thought for a few more minutes. "I've got it! Irishwood! I'm Irish and, and, it's sounds perfect to me!" Liz said jumping from her chair.

"That's great! It is perfect! I'm 40% Irish so it will work for me too. Now you just have to register your horses. And you want to do it quick before the next show comes.

Liz did what Amanda said and registered her stable and horses right away. The words, Irish Wood were all one word so there could be more room to add the rest of the horses' names. Since you could only have 24 letters to a name. Their names were: Irishwood Rock n Roll, Irishwood Sir Captain, and Guardian Angel. She had registered Angel without Irishwood, in honor of Heather. It only seemed right to Liz. Liz thought the new prefix fit the horses, and Amanda said they would be catchy in the show ring if they went. She then posted name plackets on the horse's stall doors and started looking around for different tack. With luck, Liz stumbled upon two saddles at a garage sale. She didn't know why any one wouldn't trade them at a tack store for more money. They were a great price of $152 dollars a piece. Both were in great shape as well. They were hunter saddles and could also be used for jumping.

Liz looked for a Dressage and English saddle next. She'd seen Friesians doing Dressage and thought it was beautiful. Amanda helped her learn and now Liz wanted a real Dressage saddle that would be easier to use than her trail saddle. Amanda recommended a tack store, and Liz went to it right away. Liz was really getting into the horse business and was doing things in a rush so she could look more professional.

"We have this saddle, but it's more expensive than that one," the woman said as she showed Liz the Dressage saddles.

"I think I'll take that one anyway. It was more comfortable," Liz explained. The woman nodded her head and brought the saddle to the desk.

"Is there anything else you need ma'am?" the woman asked as she looked at Liz.

"Yes. I need a double bridle and a snaffle bridle," Liz explained.

"Oh yes. Right over here," the woman said as she walked to a corner of the tack store.

Liz bought what she needed and headed for home. It seemed to take forever as she drove down the country roads and highways to get there. Finally, Liz turned her car up the little country road and came to a stop in her driveway. A happy looking Bosco greeted her as she stepped out of the car, jumping and splashing mud on her jacket.

"Down Bosco. Down," Liz said as she looked at the pup sternly. That's the trick they'd been working on lately.

Liz opened the back door of her truck and pulled out the Dressage saddle she'd bought. She walked to the tack room, which was looking more like a tack room with the other two Hunter saddles in it. She put the saddle on an empty saddle rack/holder. Liz secured it on the rack, before going back to her truck to get her double-bridle and snaffle bridle. She walked back to her tack room and hung the bridles next to the others on the pegs of the wall. Liz stepped back, only to nearly fall over Bosco who was standing behind her. Liz turned around and stepped over him, before looking at her work.

The saddles hung on their new rack, while the bridles hung from pegs on the wall. Liz smiled before walking out to the feed corner and started to scoop out the evening's feed. *This winter didn't seem to last long. It's the middle of February and there are only puddles of snow on the ground.* Liz thought as she walked into each stall, pouring the feeds in the feeding buckets. She put the carrying buckets away and headed to the hay shed.

Liz walked into Captain's stall and started to brush him. The gelding watched her carefully, he was still uneasy about being brushed in the hindquarters. Liz soothingly talked to him as she moved around his mud-covered body. The gelding eyed her every move as he ate.

"You're okay. Easy now," Liz talked to him as she reached for his tail. She took hold of it and the gelding threw his head up and stopped eating. "Easy Captain, easy boy. It's okay," Liz continued to talk to him as she worked. Liz finished grooming the horses and went into the house.

υυυ

She started the next day with another trip to the tack store. "These are the colors we have," the woman with dark hair pointed to a shelf stocked with colorful blankets.

"Thank you," Liz replied as she began to pull them one at a time and look them over. She found three nice green ones, among the others of: red, blue, orange, purple, white and black. Liz walked to the desk and paid for the blankets before returning to her car, where Bosco was waiting patiently.

"Wait 'til Amanda sees all this," Liz said as she started the car.

JUST AS GOOD

"Those were really nice blankets. You picked a good color," Amanda commented as they drove to the show. They'd been driving for nearly an hour now, and Liz was ready to get out and walk around.

"You could have brought one of your horses you know?" Amanda said as they pulled off the highway.

"They just started training," Liz said not really wanting to argue.

"But they're really good," Amanda protested.

Liz shrugged her shoulders and shifted in her seat. She turned around and looked at the horses through the window of the trailer. They had a nine-horse trailer and seven horses. The riders that were going into the show ring were in the two cars behind them. Liz looked into the trailer at the seven horses again. They had: 2 Morgans, a Quarter Horse, a Hackney, and 3 Thoroughbreds. All purebred and all very pretty.

"What classes are all these horses going into?" Liz questioned trying to figure it out, and having no luck.

"Well, we have a Hackney that will be showing in Park Carriage. Our Quarter Horse will be taking our youngest rider into a Lead-Line Class. The Morgans will be going into Saddle Seat Equitation Classes," she stopped to look for the road to turn off on, "then our Thoroughbreds will be in a Western Equitation, Hunter Equitation, and Hunter-Jumper Over Fences."

Liz sat there trying to think it all over. *How many Classes could there be?* She was trying to count in her head when Amanda sighed with relief. "We're finally here!" she said loudly as they came to the show ground gates. They paid to get in and went to park their truck. They drove to a nice little corner of the grounds. Liz stepped out of the car and took in the wonderful smell of horses, leather, and the smell of trees and grass. Liz looked around and was surprised at all the excitement at only 9:15 in the morning.

The riders and instructors from the other cars jumped out and got to work unloading and grooming the horses. Liz helped here and there, getting tack, grooming, and helping riders into the saddle. Amanda came back with cardboard like material that had numbers on them. There was one for each rider. Amanda carefully pinned the numbers to the backs of their jackets, being careful not to rip them. There were seven riders, four girls and three boys. There were a bunch of the other riders and exercise riders from the barn who came to help and cheer them on.

"Okay. Is everybody ready?" Amanda asked in a group leader voice. Everybody turned to her and shouted out an answer at the same time.

"Yes!"

"Now we talked at the barn," Amanda continued, "We don't win every time. But it's the fact that we have fun that counts. Now you guys go out there and knock 'em dead!"

"Yeh!" everybody chorused once more, before mounting or remounting their horses.

Liz and Amanda watched and helped as the riders rode around the warm up ring. Liz didn't know much about how to ride, but she did her best.

"Could you walk me and Poppy around the ring please?" a little girl asked Liz. *She's the one who's going into the lead-line class.* Liz told herself as she nodded her head. She helped the girl into the saddle and walked her around the ring. The Quarter Horse gelding walked around calmly listening to the girl's every command.

"What's your name?" Liz asked as they circled the ring for the third time.

"Jane Camie," the girl said proudly. Liz nodded her head and smiled and kept walking.

She didn't have to really lead the two around. The palomino walked calmly around, always listening to his rider. *The fact that other riders are jumping, cantering and trotting around her while she's going at a walk doesn't seem to bother her.* Liz thought as she looked at the girl who sat tall in the saddle. Liz could tell she was going into a Western class, by what she was wearing. Her hat covered her coffee brown hair. Her pink chaps and jacket showed off her palomino horse. Liz smiled and continued to lead them around.

"Jane! You're in the ring!" Amanda called as she jogged up to Liz and took the ends of the reins by the bit.

"Good luck!" Liz called as they walked toward the arena gate. Liz walked over and stood by the rail and watched as the small riders circled the ring.

"Please line up!" the loud speaker boomed. The riders and leaders came to the middle of the ring. The leaders let go of the horses, and the riders were on their own.

"In first place we have…," the loud speaker boomed out the winners for first, second, and third place. Jane didn't place in any of those.

"Now in fifth place, we have Jane Camie on Pop Around!" the loud speaker boomed. Liz clapped and hollered, as the little girl steered her big horse around to receive her ribbon.

Horse and rider came jogging out of the ring. Jane was leaning over her horse's neck, her shoulders swaying back and forth. But she lifted her head and patted Poppy's neck. She was laughing and crying.

"We did it!" she said as they walked to the trailer. She was still happy even though no one took a picture for a magazine or anything, but she was as happy as could be.

Liz sat with Amanda through the rest of the classes. *Angel can do that! Rocky could do that! And Captain could do that!* Liz said as she watched the horses enter and exit the ring. Liz realized that Amanda was right; her horses could do all these things and more! Liz couldn't wait to get home and see if she could get Angel, Rocky and Captain to do some of the things they were doing at this show.

All the riders came out with ribbons. Even if it was eighth place they were jumping with joy. Liz congratulated all of them as they exited the ring. The day came to an end, and Liz helped load the horses and get everything into the car or trailer so they didn't forget it. Liz was happy for the kids who'd ridden, and for Amanda. For Amanda had been instructing the riders, and now it had paid off.

THE AGREEMENT

"I'd love to help, and give you lessons," Amanda answered as she and Liz were driving back to Liz's ranch. Liz had asked Amanda if she'd help her get ready for a show. Amanda was more than happy, and they decided to start the next day.

"Here's your stop. See you tomorrow," Amanda said as they came to a stop in front of Liz's driveway.

"Later!" Liz called as Amanda and the trailer of horses started to move away. She went inside and got ready for the next day.

∪∪∪

"Hey stranger!" Amanda said the next morning as she jumped out of her car. Liz looked up from where she was filling water buckets by the water-spicket.

"Hey Amanda. Thanks for coming; I just have to put this in Captain's stall. Then we'll start," Liz explained. She filled the bucket and hung it on the bucket hook in Captain's stall, before going over to Amanda.

Amanda was sitting on a hay bale in the hay barn; she was throwing loose pieces of hay up in the air and watching Bosco as he tried to catch them. Liz and Amanda laughed as they sat there for a few minutes and watched the dog.

"Okay, enough. Let's get started," Amanda said as she patted Bosco on the head.

"I thought we would start with Angel. She'd be the best anyway," Liz explained as they walked to the tack-room. Amanda pulled a Hunter saddle from its rack and said, "This would be the best one to start with."

"Okay. Let's go tack up," Liz led the way back to the stall. She talked to Angel before letting herself in. She took the saddle from Amanda and lifted it onto the mare's back.

Angel stood quietly, and puffed out her stomach like other horses did. Amanda called it "sandbagging", and the horses that did it, "sandbaggers". Liz secured the saddle and slipped the bridle over Angel's head. Liz buckled the straps, and stepped back to look at the mare. Angel turned her head and shifted her weight, she was confused at what was happening and was looking for guidance. Amanda nodded with satisfaction before opening the door for Liz to walk Angel out.

"Com'on. Let's go, Angel," Liz clucked to the mare. She walked Angel out to the rectangle-shaped arena, and looked at Amanda to tell her what to do.

"Just pretend I'm not here," Amanda instructed as she stood by the mounting block to help Liz mount. Liz smiled and swung into the saddle, gathered her reins, put her feet in her stirrups and asked Angel for a walk. The Friesian mare responded willingly to the command and walked calmly around the outdoor arena.

From that point on it was work and practice. Every minute of every lesson Liz and Amanda did together. "Heels down! Back straight!" Amanda shouted to Liz as she stood on the mounting block in the center of the ring. "Get her head up and under her! That's it." It was week two and the tenth lesson for Angel, but the fourteenth for

Liz. Liz and Amanda had been working with Rocky and Captain as well. Angel circled the ring at a high stepping trot that both Liz and Amanda found she could do after the first few lessons.

"That's enough for today Liz. It's lunch time anyway!" Amanda called as Liz brought Angel to a walk.

Liz walked Angel around the ring almost six more times before Amanda said it was okay to put her out in the pasture. They usually never bothered to brush the horses if they were going to put them in the pasture, because they rolled in the mud and got dirty again. Liz took Angel's bridle off and put her forest green halter on while Amanda took the saddle off.

"Okay, she's all set," Amanda said as she patted Angel's thick black neck. Liz turned Angel and walked toward the pasture. The black mare threw her head up revealing her pure white star and gave a greeting whinny to Rocky and Captain as she entered the pasture.

"That was a good lesson," Amanda said as they started for the house.

"Thanks. It did feel good, but I had no idea there was so much involved with this riding stuff," Liz replied. They walked the rest of the way in silence. They went inside and made their own sandwiches and salads. They smiled at each other as they sat down and started to eat.

After a few minutes Amanda spoke, "Liz I have to ask you something," she hesitated. Liz set her fork down and listened. "Well you know how you and Heather worked together? Well I was wondering if we might be able to do the same," Amanda looked down at her food as she finished. Liz thought a moment, trying to understand why Amanda wanted to do this.

"Is something wrong?" Liz finally asked.

"Well, since I've been over here for the past two weeks, I'm not an instructor anymore," she hesitated as she said it. Liz fell back against the chair and thought. *I'm the reason Amanda lost her job? I had no idea.*

"Well, what I'm trying to ask is," Amanda continued, "Would it be okay if we lived together?   It would be easier for me. But I'm not sure about you."

"Well, I guess it would be okay," Liz said after thinking a minute.

"Great! But, but-" Amanda stammered, "It's just that I have four horses of my own." "You do?!" Liz couldn't believe it, "We'd have just enough stalls! It would be great!"

"Okay, all done!" Amanda and Liz said in unison as they looked at the room. It was three weeks later at the beginning of May and they'd just finished putting the last of Amanda's things in her new room at Liz's house. They'd agreed to share Irishwood Farm and everything on it.

"Now all we have to do is move the horses in and we'll be all set," Liz said as they walked into the kitchen.

"Which reminds me. I have to go get them ready and all their stuff packed too," Amanda said as she looked at her watch.

"All right. While you do that, I'll get the stalls ready," Liz replied as they now walked down the front steps.

Liz waved Amanda off before going into the house to get the piece of paper Amanda had given her. It read:

Liz these are my horses that will now be staying at our new arranged farm. (Thanks) I also registered them now that I have a name to go by.

98

Irishwood Bustin' Dust or Buster
Male Pinto: blue eyes, bay-white age 9
Irishwood Mistress or Missy
Female Pinto: blue eyes, brown-white age 6
WB My Pleasure or Penny
*Female Quarter Horse: Copper, blaze, socks on right
rear, front left and stocking on front right age11*
WB Major or Major
*Male Tennessee Walker: chocolate, front right sock age
19 (he's retired)*

*I bought Major and Penny from Willow Brook and they
already had names. Don't work too hard, but could you
please have these things done before I get there around
noon: bedded stalls, watered buckets, room for hay, and
grain, and tack.*
Thanks so much Liz!

Liz read the list twice on her way to the barn. The cool, May breeze blew against her face. She picked up the wheelbarrow and set off for the sawdust pile. Liz had a feeling that things were now officially turning for the better.

NEW FRIENDS

Liz set her breakfast dishes in the sink and hurried for the door. She pulled her favorite green sweatshirt over her head, put her warm "corral boots" on, and slipped gloves on before opening the door. It was 9:00 in the morning, the air was cold and there was still frost on the ground. Liz rubbed her hands together and opened the barn door. She said hello to everyone before giving them their feeds. She quickly gave them hay and water before checking the "To Do" list Amanda had given her.

"Okay. All I have left to do is make some space in the tack room," Liz said as she read the list.

Liz walked down the hall and into the tack room and started to stack things, along with organizing things. As she did, she felt excited. She was going to work with someone who knew just about everything about showing, riding, and proper care of all horses. Liz was working and thinking so much that she didn't realize what time it was until Amanda tapped her on the shoulder. Liz put down the brushes she was using and looked at her watch. *It's only 11:40.* Liz thought.

"I know I'm early, I thought it was going to take longer," Amanda apologized. "No that's fine. Just let me put the brushes in the drawer," Liz replied as she walked to the cabinet. She shoved them in with the rest before following Amanda out to the trailer. As soon as she got out of the barn, Liz heard a loud scream from inside the trailer.

"I arranged the stalls so that one of mine will be between one of yours," Liz hesitated, she wasn't sure if she did the right thing.

"All right. That'll be a good way for them to become friends," Amanda said as she unbolted the ramp. Liz heard the sound of metal, hooves, and neighs when a horse appeared around the corner. He was tall, but looked a bit old.

"This is Major. He's retired," Amanda explained, "You can walk him. He wouldn't hurt a flea."

Liz took the lead-rope from Amanda's hands. The horse looked at her, his dark brown eyes screamed friendliness. He searched her hands for treats before turning his head around to see everything. Liz heard her horses start a loud conversation from the barn.

"Okay let's go," Amanda said as she appeared at Liz's side with a pretty red and white Pinto. Liz smiled and led the way to the barn.

"This is Missy," Amanda said as if she sensed Liz's curiosity. As they walked into the barn, Liz's horses screamed welcomes and everything. Major turned his head and snorted, but didn't do anything else. Liz put Major in the stall in between Angel and the feed room.

"Liz, can you take Penny? Just put her in the stall next to Angel please," Amanda said as she held the lead-rope out for Liz to grab. Liz walked quickly to take it from her.

This must be the Quarter Horse mare. Liz thought as she looked at the mare's thick, rounded conformation. Liz knew that every horse was different, but Penny was a much, much different character. She pulled against the lead and breathed heavily. She was very strong as with any horse and Liz heard Amanda call from behind to just give small jerks on the lead and say easy. Liz did as she was told and Penny calmed down and listened, but was still hyper. Liz walked Penny into the barn and put her in the end stall next to Rocky, while Buster went into the stall on the other side of Angel.

Liz and Amanda sat on a hay bale outside the feed and tack room, and listened and watched the horses talk to each other.

"Oh! Did you check the stalls?" Liz asked as she remembered how they were supposed to be done.

"Yes, I checked them while I was looking for you," Amanda replied, "Thanks again for everything."

"Oh it was no problem," Liz said as she stood. "Let's go and get some lunch. We can unload the feed bags after."

"Okay. That sounds great."

Liz and Amanda walked up to the house and washed their hands at the kitchen sink.

"What should we have?" Liz asked as she looked around in the cupboards.

"Oh don't worry about that. I made a pasta salad; it's in the truck. How does that sound?" Amanda replied with a smile.

"That sounds great. I'll get the drinks and silverware if you want to go get it."

"Okay. Be right back." said Amanda as she walked out the door. Liz went to the cupboard and pulled out the silverware. She set the table before pouring milk and water into the glasses. Amanda came in with a good size bowl and set it on the counter. Without a word, they served themselves and went to the kitchen table to eat. As they ate, Amanda explained the history of each horse.

From what she was told, this is what the horses were like: Major just wanted a friend, Buster was a show-off, Missy was an adventurer and troublemaker, and Penny was a "tomboy".

"Well, from what you told me, it sounds like Missy and Buster will be hanging out with Captain. He's both of their personalities in one horse. And, if everything goes okay, Penny, Major, Rocky, and Angel might hang out too," Liz explained. They talked about the horse's personalities until they heard Bosco barking. Liz stood and walked to the door. Bosco stood by the door of Amanda's car and continued to bark. "Bosco, come!" Liz commanded. The German Shepard came jogging up, "What was that, naughty boy?"

"Actually, I was just going to talk to you about that," Amanda stepped in front of Liz. "I had 2 dogs and a barn cat. I found a home for them, but the people who took them gave them back. I tried, but no one wants them and I don't have the heart to send them to the pound." There was silence except for Bosco's whining. Liz thought a minute. *I don't know. We only have so much land and money to give. I understand the purpose, but I already gave a lot.* Liz thought and thought.

"Well let's see them," Liz said as she looked toward the truck. Amanda nodded and went down to the truck. Liz bent down and ran her hand over Bosco's smooth coat. Liz looked up again to see Amanda walking up with 2 dogs on leashes and a cat walking alongside her. Amanda had a Border Collie and a Boxer. The Collie was the usual colors of black and white, while the Boxer was Brindle with white from his toes to his knees. "They're each a year old. The Boxer is a female named Cassidy and the Collie is a male named Pepper," Amanda hesitated as she said it. Then Liz turned her attention to the palomino colored cat.

"And the cat is Chalky," Amanda said as she tried to keep the dogs under control.

Liz sat there and was swarmed with sloppy dog kisses while Bosco ran in a circle around them. Liz looked at the dog's and cat's happy faces, and then looked at Amanda's hesitant one.

"Well, if they can behave, stay out of trouble, and stay on the property, I guess they can stay," Liz said after sitting and thinking for a few minutes. Amanda smiled and gave Liz a big hug.

A NEW START

"Just follow me," Amanda said as she took hold of Liz's hand. It was the next day and Amanda had a surprise for Liz.

"Okay, open your eyes," Amanda said with a smile. Liz did as she was told and opened her eyes. Before her was her bed, but it was covered with riding clothes.

"Oh my gosh!" Liz shrieked. She walked up and felt the bottom of a pair of riding pants. Liz looked at Amanda. The woman handed her a folder with papers in it.

"They're the coggins for everybody. You can't go to the show grounds without them," Amanda explained as Liz looked through them.

"But these clothes must've cost you a fortune. You really shouldn't have done this," Liz said.

"No, no. I didn't buy them. They're mine. From when I used to show," she said looking toward the ground.

"Oh, what happened?" Liz asked as she suddenly felt sorry for Amanda.

"Well, I was in the ring with Major's half sister and a spectator threw a soda can, for whatever reason, into the arena. It hit the horse behind us," she stopped to take a breath. "The horse jumped and reared. When it did, its hooves came crashing into my back and shoulders. I fell and had a concussion. But Kitty was also hit with hooves," Amanda stopped and looked up at the ceiling. "Kitty's vertebra was broken in two places, and had to be put down. I was beaten up, but recovered. My back made it so I can't ride properly. I can ride, but not well enough to show. So I drive."

Liz stepped forward and hugged Amanda as the woman started to sob. After a few minutes she stopped and stepped back.

"Anyway. I have no use for them. I'm giving them to you as a thank you," she said with a forced smile.

"Thanks, Amanda," Liz said as she looked down at the clothes again.

"Well. What are you waiting for? Try them on," Amanda said as she stepped forward and picked up a set of Hunt Seat riding clothes and handed them to Liz.

Two and a half hours later, Liz had tried on all of the clothes. Only the shoes that went with the outfits didn't fit. But the jackets, hats, pants, and vests fit perfect. And of course, Amanda had to take pictures of Liz in every outfit, with her new digital camera. After they'd hung everything in the closet, they went outside for a ride. Amanda helped saddle Angel before setting up some walking poles, or cavaletties. Liz rode Angel over them at a walk and a trot, while Amanda stood on the mounting block in the center of the ring.

"That's enough for today Liz," Amanda called as she opened the gate for horse and rider to come through.

"I think we should lunge Rocky, Captain, and Penny today," Amanda said as she walked with Liz to the tack room.

"And maybe we should get a lesson in with Rocky and Captain," Amanda said as she hung the bridle on the rack.

"Okay," Liz said in a confused tone.

"Well, there's a show next week, just on the other side of town that we could get to. It's the Oak River show. If we gave Rocky three more lessons, he'd be more than ready. And Captain has Classic Pleasure horse written all over him. And Penny just needs a bath and we're all set," Amanda explained.

"But we don't have a cart or a carriage or whatever. And, how much time do we have?" Liz asked in a hesitant voice.

"Oh, right. But we have eleven days. That's plenty. Trust me, I've done this before. I'll register us for the show. If it's okay with you," replied Amanda as she pushed her light brown hair into a ponytail.

"Well of course it's okay with me. I mean if you really think we're ready." Amanda smiled and they both headed out to start their new project.

"It's a good thing these riding clothes were green," Liz said as she started to brush them with a cloth. The show wasn't the next day, but the day after, and Amanda and Liz were equally excited.

"I know. Green's my favorite color too," Amanda said as she picked up a hanger and put it in the closet.

"Well, when do our booked shows start?" Liz asked as she picked up a western jacket and began to polish its sequins.

"Oh. Here. Penny is the only one out of the ones we're bringing that's been to a show before," Amanda replied as she handed Liz a piece of paper in her handwriting.

The paper read:
> *9:30 Oak River Show Begins*
> *Class 14: Rocky's Hunter Pleasure Class*

Class 24: Angel's Classic Pleasure Class
LUNCH: after Class 26
Class 32: Penny's Sport horse In-Hand Class
EVENT: Foal Auction 5:40
8:00 Oakriver Show Ends

"That sounds pretty good Amanda. Have you been to the grounds before?" Liz asked as she set the paper on the coffee table.

"No. But others at Willow Brook have, and they said they were nice. And you know how they are," Amanda said as she picked up Angel's bridle and rubbed it with saddle soap.

"Yeah, I remember," Liz said. She'd never really met them, but they were high quality stables. And the people there saw themselves as high quality too.

"Oh, and we don't have to go to the foal auction if you don't want to. I just thought I should let you know it was there," Amanda said, not looking up from what she was doing.

"Thanks. I do think I'll go, and you can come too of course, just to see what's selling. I just don't understand how you could just sell a foal, or any horse, to some stranger. I know I couldn't do it," Liz said shaking her head.

"I know, I couldn't either, but I'll still go," Amanda agreed.

"Oh and I'll have to check, but my Mom has carts and carriages and lots of horse stuff. Dad used to show Morgans before his arthritis got worse. Can we go over to her house sometime after the show and see what's there?"

"Sure, that would be great. Then, if we get them, the carriages I mean, where are we going to put them?" Liz asked.

"Oh, we'll figure something out," Amanda said in her usual, positive tone. Liz couldn't believe it; all her dreams of owning horses and living "happily ever after" were coming true.

OAK RIVER SHOW

"That should do it," Amanda said in a satisfied tone as they closed the trailer ramp. It was the day of the show and both Liz and Amanda were excited. They had just finished loading horses, tack and everything else they needed and were about to hit the road.

"Oak River Show grounds, here we come!" Liz said as they pulled out of the driveway.

"Watch out world!" Amanda joked. For most of the ride there they talked about what the horses might act like.

Forty-five minutes later they pulled onto the grounds. The horses called wildly from the trailer. Liz talked to them while Amanda went to find out where their stalls were. She came back later with their show ring numbers, a schedule, and tags for the stall doors.

"Our stalls are over there," Amanda said pointing to the corner of Barn B. Amanda put the stuff she'd gotten from the show office in the car as they started to unload the horses. Amanda took Penny right to her stall, while Liz worked on calming down Angel. Liz ended up putting the chain links of the lead rope over Angel's nose to try and get her to listen.

"Easy girl. You're okay," Liz soothed Angel as they walked to the stalls. The big black mare caught everyone's eyes as they walked by. Angel pranced and gave excited snorts. Liz put the restless mare in her stall before going back to the trailer to see Rocky.

"Rocky's got 'sea legs'," Amanda said as Rocky stumbled and weaved at the end of the lead rope.

"Will he be okay to ride in his class?" Liz asked. She had never seen or heard of such a thing.

""Don't know. We'll have to wait n' see," Amanda replied as she led Rocky slowly to his stall.

Half an hour later, Rocky was still all "sea legged". Liz had walked him around a little, but it hadn't done much good.

"Well, I don't think we should take him in the class. Too much risk," Amanda said as she watched Rocky weave about in his stall. "At least we know. It's common for horses that don't travel much. He'll get better as we travel more," Amanda reassured Liz.

"Okay. As long as it doesn't last," Liz said in a worried tone.

"Don't worry, it looks worse than it is. Now let's get you and Angel ready," Amanda said as she looked at Liz.

"1, 2, 3!" Amanda counted as she gave Liz a leg up into the saddle. Class 23 was in the ring, and Angel's class had 3 entries. Liz walked Angel in circles trying to get the mare to settle down.

"Class 24: Classic Pleasure Walk/Trot, we are ready for you!" the announcer boomed. Liz took a deep breath and steered Angel toward the In Gait.

"Good luck," Amanda said as Liz rode off. People pointed and talked, stared and whispered as Liz and Angel entered the arena at a trot. Angel flared her nostrils and threw her head up as she neared the tents at the far end of the arena.

"Easy. Easy. Good…" Liz was interrupted as Angel swerved to the side as the wind fluttered the tents. Liz continued talking to her as they cut half ring.

"Walk, please!" the announcer's voice came in loud over the speakers. Angel obeyed but her steps were choppy.

The rest of the class went by in a flash. Angel and Liz had had to cut half ring the whole time, and Angel had refused to walk on the reverse.

"In First..! Second…….!" The names were called. Liz wasn't paying attention; she had all she could do to keep Angel from bolting.

"Third, we have Guardian Angel ridden and owned by Irishwood Stables!" Amanda jumped into the arena and got the ribbon before leading Angel and Liz from the ring.

Once back to the stalls, they both looked at each other and burst out laughing.

"Hey, at least the fence is still standing!" Amanda joked as Liz slid from the saddle. They untacked Angel and Amanda gave her a quick spray with the hose while Liz got undressed from her hot, sweaty Saddle Seat clothes. Liz went to the Cafeteria and grabbed them drinks and sandwiches.

"Do you like turkey?" Liz asked as they sat against the barn and unwrapped their sandwiches.

"Yeah. Is that all they had?" Amanda asked knowing that the cafeteria usually had subs.

"Yeah. It was this, tomato soup or hotdogs," Liz said as she opened her second bottle of water.

"Wow!" Liz said as Amanda walked out of the trailer in her Hunter outfit. They both had the same outfit on. Amanda had taught Liz how to lead, and she was going to be the tailor.

"It would look a lot nicer if we had matching boots," Amanda said.

"Well, they're judging Penny, not..." Liz was caught off.

"Class 32, please come to the gait!" the announcer said clearly. Liz lead Penny while Amanda walked beside the horse giving last minute wipes with her rag. Penny started to prance and strain against the reins that Liz was leading her with.

"Wait, they'll call us in by number," Amanda said as Liz started toward the gait. "We wait out here and... oops, you need to be wearing this," she clipped the "ring number" to Liz's jacket.

They were the sixth out of the eight entries to be called in. Penny trotted in with her nostrils flared and her tail in the air.

"Easy, stand. Good girl," Liz soothed as Penny squared for the judge. The judge walked around them twice, jotting down notes.

"Trot along the rail before exiting," the ringmaster told them as the judge stood back. Penny had obviously done this before. She blasted along the rail with her head high. *Amanda said this is what she was trained to do and it looks good.* Liz told herself as she ran to keep up. As they exited the ring Amanda came up beside Liz.

"That was so close to perfect," Amanda said with and ear-to-ear grin.

"What was wrong?" Liz asked knowing that it had been her fault.

"You have to stand on the side of the horse that the judge isn't on," Amanda said with a shrug. "It's okay, I hadn't told you that one."

It was ten minutes later when they finally had the results. They called everyone into the arena. Penny was happy being out in the crowds, and wasn't even noticing the tents. Amanda and Liz were so concentrated on Penny that they missed some of the placing.

"And in 5th, we have WB My Pleasure! Owned and shown by Irishwood Stables!" the announcement was made. Amanda ran to get the ribbon while Liz led Penny from the arena.

"Everything's set!" Liz called to Amanda as she went to start the truck. Liz ran and jumped into the truck and looked at the ribbons displayed on the dashboard. *Yellow and green, perfect.* Liz thought; they just seemed like perfect first colors.

"Well, I'd say that was a day of learning," Amanda said as she pulled onto the highway.

"Yes. Indeed it was," Liz agreed.

GAMES FOR ALL

It was the day after the Oak River show and Amanda and Liz planned to devote this week to the horses and dogs. They planned to get all their chores done early in the week except for cleaning stalls, so they could spend as much time with them as possible.

"The truck's cleaned out," Amanda said as Liz swept the aisle.

"Okay, could you grab that shovel and help?" Liz said as she looked at the piles of hay, shavings, and dirt.

"Sure," Amanda said as she picked up the shovel and allowed Liz to sweep the piles into the shovel before she dumped it into the wheelbarrow.

Once that was done, they turned out the horses and Liz grabbed her green rag from her desk, while Amanda got the soccer ball from the house. Liz walked out to see that Amanda had already thrown the ball and all three dogs were chasing after it. Cassidy managed to get to it first but Pepper and Bosco weren't going to give it up with out a fight.

"It sounds like they're going to murder each other," Amanda said as she walked up beside Liz.

"I know, but you can tell they're playing," Liz replied as each one managed to hold onto it and run, before losing it again.

"Well, their real hard to occupy," Amanda and Liz laughed.

"Let's see if your horses know how to play 'Green Rag'," Liz smiled, as she walked toward the pasture fence.

"Well, it sounds interesting," Amanda shrugged as she leaned on the fence. Liz gave the rag a good throw. Angel saw it and blasted forward. The other horses, especially Major, were startled and bolted away. Rocky and Captain watched as Angel brought the rag over to the fence and dropped it. Liz reached in and grabbed it, before looking at Amanda.

"I have to go get the camera! That was amazing!" Amanda exclaimed before running toward the house. Liz laughed before returning her attention to the pasture.

Angel stood there; her ears pricked forward and her big chocolate eyes shaded by her long thick forelock. *Obviously the winter's experience hadn't phased her "want to play games" spirit.* Liz thought as she studied the mare.

"Got it," Amanda came up breathlessly. She turned on the camera and focused it on the field. Penny immediately became interested. She squealed before prancing cautiously to the fence.

Liz held up the rag ready to throw, and Angel took steps back. Liz gave it a hard throw and this time Angel, Captain and Rocky were all stampeding after it. This time Rocky got a hold of it and Angel and Captain began to chase him.

"Easy Captain!" Liz called as he thrashed his hooves in Rocky's direction. Rocky threw his head up and ran for the fence where Liz and Amanda were standing. Amanda snapped pictures of everything, even of her horses who stood there and watched.

Then Missy came walking up with out hesitation and stood at the fence. Buster wanted to follow, but didn't seem as sure. Penny seemed the same as she snorted anxiously. Liz gave the rag another hard throw and all the interested horses went wheeling on their haunches after it. Missy found it hard to get, but over the next few throws she realized she didn't have to be the lady she was being trained to be.

Thirty minutes later all the horses, except Major, were fighting for the rag. Major watched with interest though as the others squealed and pushed. Then Liz felt something on the back of her leg. She turned around to find Bosco leaning against it.

"Well, that sure took it out of you guys," Liz said as the dogs lay spread out on the ground. Pepper lay with the ball at the tip of his nose.

"Well we know how to keep them occupied," Amanda laughed as she turned to look in between snapping pictures

"I think that's enough for these guys too," Liz said looking to the pasture. Angel then came up and dropped the rag. Liz smiled before picking it up and putting it into her pocket. Liz picked up the lead ropes that she had laid on the ground and opened the gait.

"It's about supper time anyway," Liz said looking at her watch. She walked Angel to the barn while Amanda followed with Buster.

"I'll get the rest of them if you want to start handing out feeds," suggested Amanda as she locked Buster's stall door.

"Okay," answered Liz. She liked bringing in the horses, but she went over to the feed corner and started dividing the grains.

Amanda came to the door ten minutes later and helped take the buckets down the aisle. Liz filled the water buckets while Amanda distributed hay. Once everything was done they said goodnight to all the horses before going to the house to see how the pictures came out.

"Well, considering that it was my first time with the digital camera, they aren't too bad," Amanda said as they look through them.

"Yeah. But you may need to work on your timing," Liz laughed as she looked at pictures of the horses flanks.

"Oh, and I talked to my Mom," Amanda said as she logged off the computer. "She said we could go up anytime we want."

"Oh good," Liz said as she started to boil some water.

"Why don't we go tomorrow?" Amanda suggested as she pulled a box of macaroni from the cupboard.

"Okay. How far away is it?" Liz asked.

"It's about forty minutes from here. So we'd want to set out between 10 and 10:30." Amanda answered.

"Okay. Why don't you give her a call to let her know," Liz suggested as she started to pour macaroni into the boiling water.

"Good idea. I'll be right back," said Amanda as she headed for the phone in the computer office.

Liz was setting the table when Amanda walked back in. She smiled before picking up the silverware.

"She said we could stay for lunch if we want."

"Well that's nice. Judging by the time we're leaving we might need to do that," Liz said, as she checked the pasta.

BOLTON STABLES

"Well this is a nice place," complimented Liz, as she got out of the car. The house was big and the color of a buckskin horse. The barn that lay to the right was a gray, cement looking building. A man and woman were standing on the porch of the house ready and waiting for them.

"Hi Mom. Hi Dad," shouted Amanda as they approached the house.

"Hi Amanda, Get here okay?" Mrs. Bolton said as she seemed to remember Heather's accident.

"Yes. This is Liz," Amanda introduced her. They were now on the porch and the Bolton's smiled warmly.

"It's a pleasure to finally meet you," Mr. Bolton said as he shook her hand. "Well, you two are welcome to look around the barn. We still have lunch to make."

"Oh don't worry. You'll probably have to remind us when it's time to come in," Amanda smiled, as she led Liz off the porch.

"If you need help, just call," Mr. Bolton called after them. Amanda nodded to them before they went into the house.

"They are very nice," Liz said to Amanda.

"I think so," she smiled. They reached the barn and opened the big doors. You could tell that it had been a very sophisticated barn when it had been used. Five stalls lay on each side of the aisle. Liz didn't have much time to observe the barn; she was too interested in what it was holding.

"That's a good idea," Liz said as she walked into a room she could tell had been the feed room.

"That's a good idea!" Liz exclaimed as she opened a garbage can where grain bags sat inside.

"So the mice don't get to them," Amanda explained as she saw what Liz was looking at.

They loaded two harnesses and three garbage cans into the back of Liz's pickup. Liz wiped her hands on her pants and continued touring the barn. She opened up what looked like a box on wheels. She found a mountain of leather halters, girths, and bits.

"Wow! Amanda, look at this!" Liz said as she started to push through some of it.

"Well, I'm not sure about the halters…" Amanda began.

"They don't have names on them," Liz observed.

"But they have memories," Amanda explained. They laid everything but the bits out on the floor.

"These are extra sets of reins for the harnesses," Amanda said as she put two of the six into plastic bags.

"Oh, this is the only halter with a name on it," Liz said as she dusted it off.

"Oh, let me see," Amanda took the halter and studied it a moment, trying to see through the dust. "Miss Lady."

"Who's that?" Liz asked tilting the halter's silver nameplate in her direction.

MISS LADY was printed in bold letters. Liz knew it was special by the look on Amanda's face.

"Daddy's first horse. He vowed never to breed her when she was born. 'Too independent' he said. That's how she got her name," Amanda hung it in the trophy case by the barn door.

"We should take them though. We could put green name plates on them," Amanda smiled. Liz helped wrap the halters and put them in the truck. That's when Mrs. Bolton called them in for lunch.

Liz took the last bite of her brownie and smiled. They'd had a chicken recipe she couldn't pronounce, and a brownie cake.

"You girls almost done with the barn?" Mr. Bolton asked as he leaned back in his chair.

"Almost. We found the halters Dad," Amanda said. "But I put Lady's in the trophy case." Mr. Bolton nodded, but it seemed to hurt to talk about her.

After setting their plates on the counter, Amanda and Liz went back to the barn. Liz walked to the back and found a second room. Something big was covered under one huge tarp. She pulled the tarp off, and found four beautiful carriages. One had green accents, and the other two had both black and brown accents.

"Oh, Amanda!" Liz called before she even felt the expensive wood.

"What..." Amanda didn't even finish before she looked at the carriages. "Oh my goodness!"

"Can we have these?" Liz didn't mean to be rude, but this had been what they were looking for.

"Yes, but I'll go let them know just to be sure," Amanda answered.

"Do we need all of them?" Liz said as she eyed the green one.

"Well. Why don't we take the green one, and if we find we need a different one, we know where they are." Amanda walked out of the barn and toward the house, while Liz made busy making room in the pickup to carry their new addition of "stuff".

"Just tie that, yes right there… good, all set," Mr. Bolton directed as they readied the green accented carriage for the drive. It was now settled in the back of Liz's pickup. And ready when they were.
"Let's see if we've looked through everything," Amanda said as she wiped her hands on her jeans. They walked toward the barn. This time Mr. Bolton came with them, and Amanda and Liz thanked him over and over. He walked through the barn as they told him what they'd looked through. Then he opened a door in the feed room that neither Liz nor Amanda had seen. He led them into the room, and Amanda and Liz were amazed at what they saw.

Piled high, was every length of lumber imaginable. Mr. Bolton looked back at the two amazed women.
"How 'bout I bring my lumber truck to the farm this coming Wednesday?" Mr. Bolton looked at his daughter.
"Sure. But Dad… I had no idea…this room…" Amanda was too bewildered to finish.
"There were times before yours my dear," Mr. Bolton hugged his daughter. Liz couldn't believe their luck. Actually, it was more like she couldn't believe the generosity that was being shown to her and Amanda.
"You'll definitely need a shed of some sort. Here's the wood to get you started," Mr. Bolton said as he smiled warmly at both of them.

THINGS CHANGE

Over the next two weeks the shed became half done. Liz and Amanda had hired a group of guys from the "store of everything", as Liz and Amanda called it. It was the size of four of the stable stalls, or was going to be. While the men were working on the shed, Liz and Angel were working on their appearance.

"That was a good lesson today," Liz remarked, as she and Amanda latched the gate of the pasture. Angel trotted off to join the rest of the herd in play fighting over the yellow jolly ball that they'd gotten from the Bolton's stable. The horses whinnied and snorted as they fought to get the toy.

"Ice tea?" Liz asked.

"That would be great," Amanda replied as they turned to walk inside. They slipped off their boots and pushed them aside. Liz got the pitcher of ice tea from the refrigerator, while Amanda grabbed two glasses from the cupboard.

"I can't believe that Angel has come this far," Liz exclaimed as she drank.

"Speaking of horses…," Amanda began.

"We're always talking about horses!" Liz laughed and Amanda shrugged and joined in.

"But anyway," Amanda started again. "I was thinking about cutting back on our herd. So we'd have more time for all of them." Liz looked shocked by the remark.

"You mean sell some of the horses?" Liz questioned.

"Yes. I was thinking maybe, Missy and Buster?" Amanda said and looked for a response from Liz.

"Well, their your horses," Liz said. She wasn't sure about the conversation.

"Well, it's just that, we would have more time for Angel and Rocky and Captain. Or Penny if we wanted to," Amanda tried to explain, as Liz nodded.

"It's just that I love them all," Liz said. She had been doing everything she could to make Amanda and her horses comfortable here. And now things had settled down and Amanda wanted to change them again.

"I know it would be hard. But didn't you feel a little bit bad that we can't spend a lot of time with some of them. And I've also gotten offers from breeding stables about Major." Amanda continued.

"Well, I understand what you're doing, but I just got settled in. So much has been changing." Liz replied as she took a sip of ice tea.

"Well, things change Liz," Amanda replied, her voice rising. Liz looked up, astounded by the comment. Liz stood up and stared at Amanda who stared back boldly.

"Don't even talk to me about change! I've changed myself and my property so many times in the past year, it's a wonder I know where everything is," Liz tried not to shout but she couldn't seem to help it.

"I'm trying to help the horses!" Amanda replied.

"I bet they just got settled in too! Especially Angel and Rocky!" Liz said pointing a finger toward the barn.

"See! You're closer to them and they're the first ones to come to your mind!" Amanda said hotly. Liz couldn't stand it a moment longer; she slammed her feet into her shoes and headed for the barn. *How dare Amanda say those things? After everything I've done for her.* Liz thought as she picked up a broom and began to sweep the aisle furiously.

She stopped every now and then to watch the horses grazing in the pasture. *Maybe Amanda was right. We have seven horses and are only riding or making time for two or three of them.* Liz turned back to sweeping the aisle. She was sweeping for another several minutes when a shadow fell upon the aisle. It was Amanda. Liz continued sweeping, acting as if Amanda wasn't there. But the aisle was clean, nearly spotless.

"Liz?" Amanda questioned. Her tone sounded like a little girl who'd just done something wrong.

"Yes. What is it?" Liz said setting down the broom and pushing a lock of hair away from her face.

"I'm sorry about what I said before. You have been changing a lot of things, including yourself over the past few months. If you don't want to sell the horses we don't have to," Amanda explained.

"No. It's okay. I understand now. Maybe we do have to sell a couple," Liz said as she looked toward the pasture. "You'd have to choose for the most part. I don't think I could do it."

"Well, I thought that Missy and Buster would be good show horses for a number of things. They're colorful Paints so children would like them a lot for a least that much," Amanda said with a smile. She'd worked with many children so she knew what they usually looked for. "And Willow Brook, the stable I came from, made an offer on Major. They'd like to use him as a breeding stallion. I figured he had lived there for eleven years so most people there already know him and I know they would treat him well." Liz thought a moment. That would leave them with Angel, Rocky, Captain, and Penny; four horses instead of seven.

"I guess. But you'd have to check the buyer's stable and property. I know squat about selling, or buying for that matter," Liz replied thinking about the three horses she had bought or gotten.

"I can do that. But are you sure you're ready for another change?" Amanda questioned. She didn't want to push Liz too far.

"As long as we really get down to working with Angel and whoever is left after we sell the others," Liz tried to bargain.

"Okay. We'll work with the four we have left every day we can," they shook hands and smiled.

After bringing in the horses, Amanda called Willow Brook. They said they'd be glad to buy him back. They would take him as soon as possible.

GOOD-BYE

It'd been three weeks since Liz and Amanda had agreed to sell Missy, Buster, and Major. Willow Brook had made a very reasonable offer for Major; he was now living there once more. Their ad for Missy and Buster had gone out three days ago; in a horse magazine and the local newspaper. Amanda had asked Willow Brook about Missy and Buster, but they had no room.

There had been one call for Buster, but the man wanted to have Buster transported to Canada to be a Birthday present for his nephew. Amanda said no, and that they wanted their horses to stay in the United States. And if it was possible, to have the horses stay in Pennsylvania. Other than being on total alert for the phone, life was normal here at Irishwood Stables. Amanda and Liz were wrestling with the dogs when the phone rang from the house.

"I'll get it," Liz said jumping to her feet and hurrying to the house. Amanda followed closely. Liz jogged into the house and picked up the phone.

"Irishwood Stables, Liz speaking. How may I help you?" Liz nearly laughed at herself. She'd answered too professionally.

"Hi. Is Amanda Bolton there, I'm calling about the two horses that are for sale," it was a woman's voice on the other end. Liz handed the phone to Amanda and walked back outside.

She went to the barn and grabbed the green towel and headed toward the pasture. And for the next twelve minutes Liz threw the towel for the horses and kicked the soccer ball for the dogs. It was different without Major's laughing snorts as he watched the others stumble and fight for the towel. Liz turned to watch Bosco, Cassidy and Pepper wrestle for the ball. They growled and bit each other, but it was only for play.

"That sounded like a nice home," Amanda said as she walked up behind Liz. "The women who just called said she has a daughter and a son who want a pony to ride. She said she also has another daughter, but she's only a year old."

"Who did you recommend?" Liz asked.

"Well, they have a stable, and the father has other livestock. The children are dedicated riders, and take riding lessons, and some day want to show. So either Buster or Missy could suit them," Amanda replied. "The woman was very talkative."

"I guess. If she told you that much just over the phone," Liz exclaimed.

"Well they're coming out in two days, Saturday, to take a look."

"We'll be ready," Liz said as they headed toward the barn.

"They're here!" Liz hollered into the house. The family who was coming to look at the horses was pulling into the driveway. Amanda set down the phone of yet another buyer and headed out the door with Liz. The family climbed out of the car and looked around. The woman had long red hair, as did her daughter. The boy had brown hair, and the father had black hair. The children started looking around in bewilderment. They'd kept Missy and Buster inside, and put the others out. Amanda led them to the barn door, and told them to wait. Liz went inside and took Missy out of her stall while Amanda talked to them.

"Hey, look!" the boy shouted as Missy emerged from the barn. Missy let the children pet and rub her while the parents looked her over. She loved the attention. After trotting her up and down the drive, Liz brought out Buster. Unlike Missy, he nosed their pockets, licked their faces and goofed off. He did this all the time and it was good for the family to see what the horse was normally like.

Liz did everything in a daze. She couldn't believe that a family might take one of these horses home. The family did know a lot about horses, and asked all the appropriate questions. Amanda explained exercise and feed for each individual horse. Amanda thanked them for coming, and the family thanked her for her time. They then got into the car and drove off.

"You hardly said anything," Amanda exclaimed as she turned to Liz.

"Well you said everything. And I just don't like the thought of some one actually buying Missy or Buster," Liz explained as she played with Angel's mane. The mare stood still on the other side of the fence and listened to the conversation.

"Well, they're going to call us tomorrow and tell us which one they'd like to buy. That was their exact words," Amanda said as she came to stand in front of Liz.

"Okay, bye," Amanda said before sitting down for lunch. "The family who came yesterday said they think Buster is a fit."

"Okay," Liz said plainly as she spooned coleslaw onto her plate.

"The father's 'livestock' is actually a herd of six donkeys. And they thought Buster's attitude would fit in. They also said he looked energetic. And that was good, for he would have to give lessons every other day."

"That sounds like something Buster would like. He likes being ridden," Liz commented.

"Yeah, I'm going to their house later. Wanna come?" ask Amanda.

"No, I'll give Buster a grooming. Maybe even ride Angel," replied Liz.

Liz watched Amanda leave the farm an hour later and started grooming Buster. But after three minutes she stopped herself. It would be harder if she spent more time with him. Instead she decided to ride Angel. The mare stood in her stall and watched Liz with her liquid brown eyes. Her Friesian black coat was clean from yesterday's grooming. Liz tacked up quickly then scribbled a note telling Amanda she was out on the trails with Angel.

Angel trotted briskly from the stable yard. The trails weren't well beaten in, but she went along without missing a beat. Liz talked endlessly to Angel about everything that was going on. They came to a large field and Liz knew the path at the other end would take them back to the west end of her property. Amanda told her not to gallop across the field; there were rodent holes that dotted the field. If Angel or any of the other horses got their foot stuck, it would probably break.

"Com'on," Liz encouraged as they loped across the field, staying close to the edge. The met the trail on the other end of the field all too soon, and Liz slowed Angel to a trot. All of a sudden, Liz's cell phone started to ring. The shrill noise made Angel leap and jump around. She whinnied and bolted in different directions. Liz flipped the phone open and the ringing stopped.

"Hello!" Liz shouted, angry at whoever had called and spooked Angel.

"It's Amanda. What's wrong?" Amanda's voice was filled with worry.

"I'm riding Angel. Why'd you call me? The ringing scared her and I'm trying to calm her down," Liz said trying not to shout again. She rubbed Angel's shoulder, now the mare was just looking back at Liz to see what was going on.

"You're suppose to put your cell phone on vibrate when you ride," Amanda reminded Liz.

"Forgot," Liz replied, just remembering.

"That family, the Rensey's, want to buy Buster and they have the perfect place for him," Amanda said excitedly.

"That's great," Liz replied a little sad. By now, she and Angel were walking along the path again.

"I also called and canceled the ads for Buster, but three people called about Missy. Only one sounded good. I think we should check it out. I can't believe so many people are interested and called," Amanda said, sounding amazed. Liz looked down, she was about to cry.

TOO PERFECT

Liz walked to the house. She had just finished grooming Angel from their trail ride. Amanda was nowhere in the kitchen or living room. Liz walked down the hall and found her in the office, starring at the computer screen.

"Hi. How was your ride?" Amanda asked, not even taking her eyes off the screen.

"It was good," Liz replied. She looked over and read the headline at the top of the screen. HELPING HOOVES, it read.

"What are you reading?" Liz questioned as she tried to figure out this puzzle.

"Oh," answered Amanda as she turned her attention to Liz. "The people who called about Missy were from Helping Hooves. They said to check out their site, and I think she might be what they're looking for."

"Really?" Liz asked, not sure how to feel.

"They're looking for a calm, sturdy, 'doesn't spook at anything horse' and that's pretty much what Missy is. Didn't you see her with the Rensey's children?" Amanda looked at Liz's fallen face and invited her to the kitchen for coffee.

"The Rensey's ranch was beautiful. They had big pastures, roomy stalls, plus it was clean and healthy. It was perfect," Amanda continued, as she set down a full coffee mug in front of Liz. *Too perfect*, Liz thought as she sipped her coffee.

"What is Helping Hooves?" Liz asked Amanda.

"Oh, it's an equestrian therapy center for children with diseases like Cerebral Palsy and other disabilities. Missy would fit in, at least I'm pretty sure she would," Amanda said.

"Sounds like it. Are we going to go meet the people or kids?" Liz asked guessing that Amanda had that worked out already.

"Well, I was going to ask them to come tomorrow," Amanda said, asking more than explaining.

"That would be fine," Liz said, looking at the table.

"Are you sure you're okay?" Amanda asked.

"It's just that I didn't think there would be people interested in our horses this fast. Well, it's that I realized that these people are offering our horses better things than we could," Liz finished; she looked at Amanda, her eyes filled with sympathy.

"But we are offering them the best. We're letting them move on to start doing things they love. We're making that happen," Amanda explained. While Liz felt like a child, she didn't feel so bad now.

ᴕᴕᴕ

The next morning, Liz was up early, riding Angel. She rode her in the ring this time. The mare moved gracefully around the rail. Liz felt wonderful, she didn't want to stop, just go on, and on. Yet she had to; the children would be there in an hour and she had to help Amanda set up.

The children were going to be here most the day. Liz had to get the stable ready, while Amanda set up a refreshment/lunch table off to the side. Liz untacked and

GUARDIAN ANGEL

gave Angel a quick, but good grooming. She had to
decide where to put the horses: in the pasture behind the
barn, or the pasture that lined the driveway. She decided
to put everyone but Missy in the pasture behind the barn.
She would put someone out with Missy, but she didn't
know what Amanda had planned. Cassidy and Pepper
dozed in the grass; while Bosco watched Liz and each
horse go to the pasture. He stood guard over imaginary
territory. Liz laughed and went to Missy's stall.

"Hey pretty girl. Some ones coming to look at you
today," Liz said as she brushed the mare with a body
brush. "There are gonna be a lot of kids, don't be scared,
just be Missy."

"Liz! They're here," Amanda called from the yard. Liz
walked out and saw a large van making its way up the
driveway. "I'm going to let the adults see Missy in the
barn first," she instructed.

Pretty soon the yard was filled with noise, yet
Missy stood with her head over the door. She watched
intently, Liz had a feeling this was her future family.

"This is Liz," Amanda's voice brought Liz back to
reality. "Liz this is Karen Stanza."

"Nice to meet you," Liz shook Karen's hand. Liz then
turned her attention to the children. Two of the twelve
were in wheelchairs.

"Liz will show you to Missy's stall. We'll bring her to
the yard and pasture in a minute," Amanda said as she
took the hands of one of the children. Liz led the way.
She told Karen about Missy and how she was sturdy and
calm; that the Paint would do just about anything asked
of her.

A few minutes later, Karen was hugging and brushing Missy while Amanda talked to the children. Liz stayed with Karen, answering questions.

"Can we bring her outside? I want to see how she'll react around the children," Karen said with a smile. Liz clipped a lead rope to Missy's halter and led her outside. The children jumped, screamed, and made many other noises. Missy looked at them with a startled eye, but kept quiet. Karen and Amanda held the children in their arms, so they could pet Missy. Missy stayed quiet and seemed to love the attention.

Just as Liz went to put Missy in the pasture, a little girl ran up and grabbed Missy's hind leg. The mare threw her head in the air and stepped forward, but stayed calm. Amanda, Liz and Karen looked shocked.

"She's amazing," Karen commented as she scooped the little girl into her arms. Liz smiled, and Amanda continued talking with Karen and the children. Liz led Missy to the middle of the pasture and unclipped the lead. The mare trotted in a circle before stopping to graze.

The next hour went in a whirl. Liz was picking up the lunch table, when Amanda came to talk to her.

"Karen thinks Missy is perfect for the program. She made an offer," Amanda stopped short when Liz looked up." It's not as much as we were looking for, but I think Missy would be very happy with them."

"I think so too," Liz said with a smile.

"It's just, they were wondering if they could bring her home today," Amanda's voice was quivering. Liz bit her lip, not ready for the information.

"It's the children, they're so upset, they really love her," Amanda tried to explain.

"I know. If they are totally ready, Missy can leave in an hour," Liz answered. Amanda jumped up in the air.

"Thank you, for everything. I know this is hard," Amanda said as she hugged Liz. "I'll go tell Karen."

Liz watched as the children stood around Missy in the pasture. The two volunteers and Karen watched them carefully. Amanda walked into the field and started talking with Karen. But Liz was watching Missy. The girl, who had jumped on her leg, was patting the mare's broad chest. Missy lowered her head, putting her forehead against the girl's. *It's too perfect, like a fairy tale.* Liz thought. This is what Missy liked doing: a calm, quiet life, being loved and caressed.

TOGETHER

Colored leaves dotted the yard as Liz led Angel from the stable. It was mid September. It'd been a month since Missy and Buster had left, and now Liz and Amanda concentrated on getting the horses they had, trained and ready for whatever show might come their way. Liz led Angel while Amanda stood at the gate of the riding ring. Pepper whined from his place at the barn. Amanda had tied them to the outside of the stable so they couldn't interfere with the lesson.

"What are we going to work on today?" Liz asked as she brought Angel to the mounting block.

"Well, I thought that we'd practice bringing her nose in and then we'd go on a trail ride," Amanda said as she held Angel's head while Liz swung into the saddle.

"Trail ride?" Liz questioned. "I thought... Your accident..."

"Oh don't worry. I can ride. I just sit awkwardly. I'll ride Penny," Amanda said reassuringly. Liz turned Angel toward the rail at a trot. Amanda gave instructions, and Liz tried to follow them.

"See-saw the reins... there you go," Amanda watched as Angel's head moved up and her nose bent in toward her chest. Liz did this at a walk and at a trot, and Angel performed well considering it was something new.

"Okay, that's enough for today. I'll go get Penny," Amanda said as she let herself out of the ring. Liz dismounted and rubbed Angel's forehead. Her white star was tan now, even though Liz brushed the Friesian every other day.

"Ready?" Amanda questioned. She led Penny into the ring and up to the mounting block. Amanda did mount and ride awkwardly. Her legs were pushed back; her shoulders weren't squared with Penny's. Liz smiled and swung back into Angel's saddle. Then, as they rode from the yard, Amanda grabbed a handful of the mare's mane and set her hands, slightly below Penny's withers. Liz ignored it and trotted beside Penny. They trotted down the trail in silence. Only the horse's hoof beats and breathing and the sound of crunching leaves broke it up.

"Amanda, how come you didn't ride Rocky? He's just calmer," Liz asked as she watched Penny pull at the bit and pull her rider around.

"Well, Penny is like this, but if something happened, she's trained to stay by my side. And she was my therapy horse. The only one I rode. They decided to sell her because she wasn't too calm. I thought she was great, and I can control her and she doesn't seem to mind my awkward riding," Amanda didn't seem shy to talk about it. Then again, Amanda wasn't shy with anything.

They came to the field and let their horses canter along the perimeter. Angel cantered smoothly, but Penny wanted to go faster. They soon came to a rest and Liz told Amanda to wait here with Angel and Penny as she dismounted and walked into the woods. It was still her property. On the other side, was a massive field, more like a meadow. There was a steep hill on the left, but it didn't matter much. This had been her father's cornfield. There wouldn't be any rodents' burrows here. She turned and ran back to Amanda.

"My father's corn field! We can ride and gallop and race there," Liz said excitedly.

"The brush is too thick for the horses," Amanda explained as Liz mounted Angel. The mare started walking toward the brush.

"Easy girl, this way," Liz soothed as she tried to turn the mare around. Angel walked toward the brush, and pawed furiously.

"Easy, easy," Liz tried to calm the big mare, but it wasn't working. Then Liz saw it. There was a narrow path through woods. Just big enough for a horse to squeeze through.

"Look what Angel found!" Liz exclaimed as Amanda rode up on Penny. They squeezed along the path until they reached the meadow. Amanda looked around in amazement.

"I didn't know all this was back here," Amanda said as she tried to keep Penny from bolting.

"Com'on!" Liz shouted as she nudged Angel in the sides and the mare broke into a canter. Amanda followed closely on Penny. Before long they were galloping across the meadow.

"That was amazing!" Amanda said as they walked into the yard. They untacked and gave their horses a long grooming. Liz used the body brush on Angel's ebony, Friesian coat. Angel nearly fell asleep.

"What are we doing for tomorrow's lesson?" Liz asked as she and Amanda dished out evening feeds.

"I don't know? Probably just work on what we did today a little more," Amanda said as she headed off down the hall with three feed buckets. When she wasn't on a horse,

Amanda was normal. Her strides were long and steady; she walked straight, with her shoulders squared.

Once the feeds were done, Liz gave Rocky a long grooming, while Amanda groomed Captain. Rocky seemed more energetic then usual.

"I haven't ridden you in a while, huh boy?" Liz said as she rubbed Rocky's forehead. The gelding pushed into it, nearly knocking Liz over.

"Liz? You ready for our supper?" Amanda said with a smile.

"Sure," Liz put the brushes back in the tack room and joined Amanda in the kitchen.

Amanda had been stirring soup, and was just turning off the stove, as Liz walked in. Liz took two bowls from the cupboard. Amanda spooned the soup into the bowls, and then they both went to the living room and watched TV. They watched ANIMAL PLANET and the news before going to bed. Liz said good night and watched as Amanda went into the extra bedroom. Liz changed into her pajamas and laid down in her bed. She finished *Sea Star* for what seemed the fiftieth time. She turned out her light and went to sleep.

ᴜᴜᴜ

She dreamed of riding down the rail of the show ring. She was mounted on Angel; the mare had a bow of ribbons on her shoulders and a ribbon clipped to her bridle. Liz smiled as every one snapped pictures as she and Angel trotted down the rail. The crowd cheered as the loud speaker boomed words, Liz couldn't understand, for Angel's hoof beats and snorts were all she could hear.

A shrill noise awoke Liz. She turned to see it was Bosco. He, along with Cassidy and Pepper, wanted to go outside.

"Guys. It's... 6:12, I'll get up," Liz stumbled out of bed and to the front door. The dogs fled and started wrestling and playing with the soccer ball. Liz smiled and put on pot of coffee. She heard Amanda shuffle from down the hall. She was probably going to the office to order feed or something.

"Liz! Look at this" Liz heard Amanda holler a couple of minutes later. Liz walked into the office and looked at where Amanda pointed on the computer. Liz couldn't believe what she saw. It was Missy!!!

"Oh my God! She's the center of attention," Liz said as she scrolled down the pictures. Kids sat on Missy, led her around, and brushed her. The mare seemed happy and content in every picture.

"I'm sorry I didn't get to know these people better," Liz said as she sat in the chair of the desk. She suddenly felt guilty that she hadn't gotten to know the buyer better. Liz read the descriptions beneath the pictures, and was comforted to know that at least one of the horses was doing fine.

CLOSE CALL

Liz posted to Angel's graceful gait as they trotted around the rail of the riding ring. Angel tossed her head and brought her nose to be perpendicular to the ground. Amanda smiled and waved them over.

"I think we'll have to go trail riding tomorrow. It's getting dark, and now that it's autumn it's going to get dark quicker," Amanda explained as she rubbed Angel's forehead.

"Okay," Liz said understandingly as she slid from Angel's broad back. Liz walked Angel to the barn and untacked her while Amanda started filling water buckets. She groomed Angel to perfection.

Liz then walked to the feed room and dished out feeds for each horse. Amanda groomed Rocky and Captain as Liz finished giving out hay before they both went inside.

Amanda served the pot roast she'd gotten ready that morning and they both went into the living room. They turned on the news and watched as the reporters quickly narrated each story. But one caught their eyes and ears.

"And we are warning citizens on the outskirts of Scranton to stay alert. There have been reports of illegal hunters trespassing on properties," the reporter announced. After switching to the weather, Amanda and Liz stared at each other for a moment.

"We lived here for years and that's never happened," Liz reassured, as she stood and set her plate in the kitchen for the dogs to clean.

"Yeah, but we have horses. People get a lot of money for horsehair and meat. And the whole horse for that matter," replied Amanda not sounding assured.

"We have "No Trespassing" signs. So they couldn't say they made a mistake, they shouldn't be hunting here at all. Who said they were coming in the direction of Irishwood stables anyway," Liz wasn't too worried. There was a very slim chance of it.

Liz turned out the light in her bedroom and fell asleep. She thought about the progress she was making with Angel and couldn't wait for the next lesson. Liz slept soundly. She had the same dream of riding around the show arena. She and Angel were the champions.

∪∪∪

"You ride ahead, I have to fix my stirrup leather," Amanda said as she slid from Rocky's back. They were on a trail ride and were in Liz's father's cornfield. Amanda had decided to ride Rocky today and give Penny some playtime with Captain, and this gave Captain a new playmate. Liz turned Angel and rode toward the wooded side of the field.

"Easy," Liz said as Angel pulled at the bit. All of a sudden, Angel stiffened like a board. She flared her nostrils and looked toward the woods.

"What's wrong, pretty girl?" Liz asked and tried to urge the Friesian mare forward. Angel screamed and jumped around. Rocky spun and Amanda stayed on the ground to control him.

"Easy! Calm down!" Liz tried to soothe the frightened mare, but she was unsuccessful. The mare bolted into the woods. She spun and screamed. Then she stopped, her body still tense. She flicked her ears in all directions. Something rustled behind them and Angel spun in its direction and screamed. She then kept snorting and jumping.

Liz heard Amanda's faint call from the meadow. Something rustled, clicked and snapped. Angel jump, gave a series of half rears, snorted and continued to spin in circles. Stopping for only a second to listen and look. Then Angel spun and stood stock-still. Her ears pointed in the direction of a fallen tree. Then Liz saw and was horrified by it. She talked without knowing it. Trying to calm herself, just as much as she was Angel.

Slowly, a man with a rifle rose and stared at the horse and rider. Amanda was in the meadow, but could see faintly what was going on. Rocky tugged at the reins and snorted, but the man paid attention to the big black mare. He prepared to shoot. Angel reared; Liz hung on with all her strength. The mare jumped around then bolted toward the rifleman. He scurried around, trying to shoot and avoid flying hooves. By now, Liz was scared out of her mind; she tried to stop the raging mare.

"Easy, Angel! Stop! Angel Please!" Liz's words went unheard by the angry mare. Liz saw two other men stand up and point rifles at her and Angel. Angel saw this too and herded them together best she could and struck out with hard, sharp hooves.

The men shouted amongst themselves. There was a gunshot and Angel charged. She knocked two of the men into one another and chased the other. Liz caught a glimpsed of Amanda and Rocky. The Mustang must've had dozens of flashbacks from his time in the wild. While Amanda held a cell phone to her ear and her lips moved frantically, Rocky spun and jumped and the chaos continued.

Another gunshot sent Angel into a bigger rage than before. She knocked two of the men under the fallen log. The other lay holding his wrist. Three shots were fired and Angel pounded the log and screamed. The man who wasn't under the log pointed his rifle at the black mare and fired. Angel looked up and ran toward him. *He'd missed!* Liz knew that Angel would've screamed if he'd hit her. Liz's feet fell free of the stirrups and she squeezed with her knees for life. The thunder of Angel's hooves, and the lightening of her screams and snorts echoed in Liz's ears. She fought to stay on, as the mare fought three men with rifles. She did this without throwing her rider and putting her in danger.

"Don't get hurt!" Liz whispered as Angel whirled about. Then out of nowhere, a siren sounded and the next thing Liz knew, she was surrounded by Police Officers. They took the riflemen in the police cab and drove them away. Amanda talked with the sheriff, while others tried to get Angel under control. The mare bolted away and Liz got off and led her back.

"You are the greatest. You saved me," Liz smiled and halted the mare and cried into her mane. The police couldn't see her from here. Liz murmured to Angel and Angel listened intently.

"Com'on. They won't touch you," Liz reassured as they came toward the police crowd again.

"Stay back please. I'll handle the mare," Liz announced, and the officers backed away.

"Thank you officer," Liz said as he walked out of the barn. She ran to Angel's stall. The mare looked up; she was lying on the floor.

"You're tired as anything," Liz said as she knelt beside the mare and stroked her sweat-dried coat with her hand. An hour later, Amanda came in, draped a blanket around Liz and brought her inside.

"I did the feeds, and you and Angel just need a lot of rest," Amanda said as they entered the house.

∪∪∪

Liz lied in bed and tried to sleep. When she did fall asleep, she had a dream.

"Heather?" Liz questioned. She was in the clouds; she walked toward the floating figure.

"Everything you said has happened," Liz explained, hoping that would end her fears and anxiety.

"She will do the acts many times. They will come more often. Some acts will happen more than others. Believe!" Heather disappeared and Liz sat up in bed. Her back ached, as well as her head. *I guess I'm not out of the woods yet.* Liz fell back to sleep, but didn't dream anymore.

RECOVERING

Liz sat up slowly. It'd been two days since the event in the cornfield forest. Liz stood and cringed as a pain shot through her back. She got into the shower and took a long hot one. She dressed and went into the kitchen. She grabbed one of the muffins that Amanda had made earlier and went out to the barn. Amanda was grooming Captain as Liz entered. Angel whickered and pawed the ground as Liz walked toward her stall. This would be the first time she'd seen Angel since the night after the attack. The mare moved as stiffly as Liz, but seemed happy. Liz then saw how big Angel was. She was 15.3 hands, thick boned and powerful. Liz knew she would've been terrified if Angel had attacked her like she had the men two days ago. Liz hugged the mare and talked to her, her words soothing both of them.

Liz took the muffin from her pocket and split it with Angel. The mare ate it greedily and looked for more.

"Did you feed them already?" Liz asked, turning to Amanda.

"Yeah," Amanda answered as she untangled a knot in Captain's mane. Liz nodded and picked up a body brush. She brushed Angel's silky, black coat until it shone. Amanda had moved on to Rocky and Liz was still brushing Angel. She felt kind of selfish, she was just brushing one horse and Amanda was brushing the rest of them on her own.

"It just seems selfish," Liz said as she wove her fingers through Angel's mane.

"What does?" Amanda asked with a puzzled look.

"Oh, well, it's just," Liz stammered as Amanda listened for an answer. "Well, you're brushing everyone and I'm just brushing Angel."

"It's fine. She's obviously special to you, and you should form a special bond with her. Rocky loves everyone. And Captain, if I'm the only one that's going to drive him then he should learn about me," Amanda explained with an understanding smile.

"Thanks," Liz said. She was glad she didn't have to try to divide her time right now. Liz smiled and continued brushing Angel's coat. As soon as it glistened with health, Liz sat on the bale of hay out in the barn aisle.

"Let's go inside. It looks like it's going to rain and you need some more rest," Amanda said as she saw the dark circles under Liz's eyes. Liz was too tired to argue and followed Amanda into the house.

Liz sat on the coach and spooned soup into her mouth. Amanda hurried around the house: cleaning, talking on the phone, feeding the dogs, and looking after Liz. *I'm so lucky to have a friend like Amanda*, Liz thought as she watched the young woman. Before Liz knew it she was asleep on the coach.

"Liz? Liz," Amanda tried to wake up her friend. Liz opened her eyes, sat up, and rubbed them.

"Feel better?" Amanda set a cup of tea in front her. Liz tried to stand, but found it difficult, not as hard as before, but difficult.

"My back's still stiff and my arms and legs are sore. Liz rubbed her shoulders and pushed her hands to her spine. Amanda helped her to the shower before going out to the barn. Liz enjoyed the warmth and soothing of the water as it flowed from the showerhead. *Angel would probably love a bath like this too,* Liz thought as she washed her face. Once out of the shower she went to the kitchen and started dinner. She decided to make homemade vegetable soup. She knew her mother's recipe by heart, and didn't need any cookbook to remind her. She chopped up the carrots and got everything ready for the soup before setting the table.

She stopped and looked at the kitchen clock, it said it was 5:28pm. She washed her hands and looked out the kitchen window. Amanda was walking up the path to the house. Liz then heard the teapot scream and went to take care of it.

"Something smells good," Amanda said taking a big whiff of the aroma that wafted through the kitchen.

"I made my mother's special vegetable soup. I hope you like it," Liz said with a smile.

"Oh, if it smells this good, I'm sure I'll love it," Amanda said excitedly, as she washed her hands. Liz dished out the soup and they sat at the kitchen table and ate.

"I think Captain's ready to start in carriage. We could start tomorrow," Amanda said as she spooned soup into her mouth quickly.

"But I don't know anything about driving. I thought you were going to train and maybe show him," Liz said. She knew nothing about carriages, carts, or the difference between them.

"Oh, okay. I guess you could do some work with Angel. Although she's pretty sore," Amanda said as she helped herself to more soup.

"I'll just brush her and walk her on a lead. She could use a vacation anyway," Liz said before helping herself to another serving as well.

∪∪∪

Liz drew the brush across Angel in long strides. The mare enjoyed it, but looked toward the pasture.

"We'll walk once around the yard and then you can go in the pasture," Liz set her brushes down and hooked a lead to Angel's halter. The mare walked stiffly from her stall and out into the yard. Amanda stood in the arena with Captain, getting the pony used to the monster that he would soon pull.

"Walk," Liz commanded as she and Angel started down the drive. Halfway down Liz brought Angel to a jog. The mare was still stiff and they fell back to a walk quickly.

"All right. To the pasture," Liz agreed as Angel tugged in that direction. Liz unclipped the lead and the mare trotted stiffly toward Rocky and Penny and chased them away, with flattened ears, from the clover patch they'd been munching on.

"Witch," Liz said jokingly under her breath as she watched as Angel established her place at the top of the pecking order. Amanda talked and stroked the little Pindos pony as she tried to urge him closer to the carriage. The pony took a hesitant step and Amanda rewarded him with a praising word and a stroke on the neck.

Captain was then led in circles around the carriage and came closer each time. Liz was happy to see everything so peaceful. She enjoyed it, for she knew it wouldn't last very long. She looked glumly toward the barn and started for the wheelbarrow. Amanda had done them the last three days, so it was her turn. She rolled the wheelbarrow down the aisle. *Heather must've helped me recover.* *It went way too quick,* Liz thought as she felt a lot less pain in her back. She smiled gratefully and started shoveling soiled shavings into the wheelbarrow.

CHILL OF WINTER

The ground was covered in a blanket of leaves and a blanket of snow as well. There was less than an inch, but winter was definitely here. The cold air was accompanied by a crisp, bone-jarring wind. Liz blew into her gloved hands as she waited for the water spicket to fill the water bucket. Amanda rolled a large cart down the barn aisle that they now used for carrying hay from stall to stall. Penny pawed and paced, for she only got a handful of grain and two flakes of hay. Liz called it being an "easy-keeper".

"Finally," Liz sighed as she lifted the full water bucket and hurried down the hall. It was evening feedings so everyone would need water. They hadn't gone outside today; the wind had been too fierce and icy. She went to Captain's stall and refilled his water bucket, then Penny's. By that time Amanda had another ready. Liz quickly filled Rocky's bucket and then went to Angel's stall, but Liz was surprised. Angel had barely drunk any water; she had only nibbled on her hay, and hadn't touched her grain. Liz rubbed the mare's neck, but instead of pushing into her grooming, Angel shifted uncomfortably.

"What's wrong pretty girl?" Liz asked, but Angel only turned her head away. Liz set the bucket outside the stall and put her hand on Angel's chest. It was burning! Liz pulled her hand away quickly and left the stall. She jogged to the barn office and found Amanda cleaning brushes.

"Angel has a fever. Or at least I think she does. I'm going to take her temperature," Liz opened the desk draw and pulled out the thermometer. Amanda helped her as they went to Angel's stall.

"Oh my God!" Amanda exclaimed.

"What? How bad?" Liz asked anxiously as she held Angel's head.

"She has a temperature of 104," Amanda said looking horrified. "The medicines we have aren't nearly strong enough, we'll have to call the vet," Amanda said as she put a hand on Angel's neck. Liz looked at her watch and sighed.

"The clinic closed an hour ago," Liz said, as she felt helpless and bad for letting Angel get into this state.

"I can give her what we have, that will hold her over until tomorrow morning," Amanda suggested.

"I guess we don't have a choice. We'll do our best Angel," Liz said. Amanda used a syringe to get Angel to take the medicine. Liz would've stayed and brushed her, but the mare seemed sore and uncomfortable and wanted to rest.

Liz said a prayer that night. She felt she was getting too worried and uptight about the situation, but she couldn't help it. She slid into bed and hoped tomorrow brought better news and health with it.

υυυ

The only thing the next day brought was a snowstorm. The snow and wind worked together to destroy everything. Liz and Amanda ate breakfast quickly then bundled up. Scarves, gloves, heavy jackets, and hats, they could barely breathe. They looped arms and set off toward the barn. They had to help each other stand as the wind blasted at them. Liz reached the barn door, it was almost frozen shut. They both pried it open and squeezed through. The horses looked up anxiously for their breakfast. Liz went straight to Angel's stall. The mare didn't look any better, but she didn't look worse either.

"Call right away, and I'll feed the rest of them and give them something to stay quiet and drowsy," Amanda said. The horses hadn't been outside in three days and were very hyper.

"Trust me you don't want to go outside," Liz hollered to them as she hurried to the barn office. After she hung up she went to find Amanda.

"The vet is on his way and said to leave her alone till he gets here," Liz explained as Amanda shrugged her shoulders. Liz went down the aisle and started filling water buckets.

It seemed like an eternity, but the vet finally arrived. It always seemed like it took forever for the vet to get here.

"I'm Conrad. I've been here before but I don't remember you," Conrad said as they helped brush the heavy snow from his shoulders. He pointed to Amanda before shaking her hand.

"I'm Amanda," Amanda answered. Liz led Conrad to Angel's stall. Angel lifted her head and shifted away as Conrad and Liz entered. Amanda stood in the doorway of the stall. Liz bit her lip as Conrad quickly started looking the mare over. He took her temperature, blood pressure and wrote it down on his clipboard.

"I can give her antibiotics, but all I know is that she has a fever and a kind of cold," Conrad explained. "Easy, girl," he ran his hand down her face and looked into her eyes and nostrils. He left the stall followed by Liz.

"Has she eaten anything today?" Conrad asked looking at Liz.

"No. Well, a nibble of grain and hay, but no water," Liz was hesitant to see what Conrad would say next.

"Give her this twice a day, at least seven hours apart. And if you want I can come back and draw blood for further inspection if she doesn't improve. Don't give her any today, because I just gave her a dose of antibiotics. Anything else," Conrad asked as he handed Liz and Amanda a couple of syringes filled with medicines.

"How long do we give this to her?" Amanda asked. They had enough in there hands to last four days.

"Till it's gone. If she still has a temperature tomorrow, give a call," Conrad nodded a goodbye, before leaving and braving the wind outside. Liz walked back to Angel's stall.

"Try to rest n' get better," Liz crooned to Angel. The mare flicked her ears and tilted her head, but stood still.

"It shouldn't be anything too serious," Amanda said as they ate their soup at the kitchen table.

"But it's just that when I bought her from the auction, I didn't want her to think and act of me the way she did Jake. That was his name right?" Liz explained, then asked. Amanda nodded her head and put her bowl on the kitchen floor so the dogs could lap up what little was left.

Liz fiddled with her glass of water and couldn't help but feel that it was her fault Angel was like this.

ALMOST OVER

"This is the last one. Com'on," Liz crooned as she tried to get the syringe into Angel's mouth. This would be the last time Liz had to do this. Angel curled here lips as Liz pulled the now empty syringe from her mouth. Liz laughed and patted Angel's neck. The mare was back to her old self and pushed into her grooming. Liz stumbled back a few steps.

"These heated buckets work real well," Amanda exclaimed as she filled Penny's.

Christmas had been a month ago!

"Time flies!" Amanda had said on Christmas Eve. It hadn't been a very traditional one: they had a four-foot tree, twenty ornaments, and there had been a total of seven presents under the tree. Liz had gotten a helmet, helmet cover, and a sweater with running horses on the front. Amanda had gotten a new helmet, gloves and hats with horse heads on them, and a gift certificate. Then the Bolton's had sent them the seventh gift; it was a huge package that had been filled with eight heated water buckets. Liz and Amanda had screamed thanks into the phone. The Bolton's said they missed shopping for stuff like that, and wanted to do whatever they could to help. It had taken Liz and Amanda four days to install the ones they needed.

Liz's birthday had also come and gone. It was the day after that they'd noticed and had a mini celebration, with cookies substituting for cake. Amanda had given her a hug and the promise of a safe trail ride as presents. Now it was February 4th, and the land was a muckheap. Most of the snow had melted and turned the green, lush pasture into an ocean of slick mud and rivers of slushy water.

But the forecast said this might as well be spring. There were no further storms; just snow flurries and light rain showers. Liz and Amanda didn't take it for granted and kept the horses inside. Everybody but Angel was furious and energetic. Angel was doing well, no fever or anything. Yet she was exhausted from fighting off the sickness. Liz stroked her face and murmured to Angel and the mare bowed her thick, muscled neck in enjoyment.

"Liz, I think we should check the pasture. These guys are gonna put holes in the wall soon," Amanda said with a laugh. Penny paced, Rocky pawed, and Captain was just plain restless. Liz nodded and walked with Amanda to the pasture.

"I want to try to work Angel everyday come warm weather and dry ground. I want to start showing a lot this year," Liz explained.

"Okay. Captain will be ready soon too," Amanda replied. They reached the gait and split up. Amanda went to the left and Liz went to the right.

They met at the far end of the pasture and decided it wasn't dry enough. The horses would have to wait a few more days.

"We could lunge them in the yard. It's padded down dirt like the driveway, it'll be fine," Liz suggested, and then confirmed.

"That's a good idea. I think we should lunge Penny first. Then Rocky and Captain," Amanda looked into the barn and watched the restless horses.

Rocky bolted and galloped in a wide circle around Liz. He bucked and jumped and went crazy at the end of the lunge line. Liz held tight to the end and let the Mustang get his built up energy out. He was far enough away so he wouldn't hurt her, and could still do basically the same thing he would do in the pasture. Liz and Amanda laughed while Rocky just continued his gallop. *My special boy. My first horse.* Liz thought as she remembered that day at the auction. Now, almost two years later, she had the two most special horses; she would never let them go. Rocky would continue galloping, bucking, and trotting around on the lunge line for another twenty minutes before he calmed to a walk.

Liz followed Amanda with Captain, into the barn. Angel stood dozing in her stall. Amanda and Liz spent the rest of the day cleaning the barn and the house. When feeding time came, Liz filled buckets and Amanda fed them with grain and hay. Liz entered Rocky's stall and started to groom him. She bent down and started to clean his feet.

"Pick it up," Liz said. When Liz said it again, she leaned into his shoulder, and squeezed his fetlock bone. Rocky lifted his foot and they went though the rest without a fuss.

"Liz, we need to get the farrier out here," Amanda said as she came out of Penny's stall. "Their feet are getting long n' weird shaped."

"I'll call once we're inside," Liz said as she looked at Angel's hooves. They could use a trimming too. Liz and Amanda finished up in the barn and went into the house.

OOO

"Stand," the farrier's voice was firm, but Captain jumped forward and rolled the whites of his eyes. He obviously didn't like farriers in general; he'd most likely had a bad experience. It seemed everything went that way for Captain. Amanda murmured to him, held him steady, and Captain seemed to calm a little bit. The farrier lifted the last hoof, cleaned it, trimmed it and set it down as fast as he could. Captain was the last one; the others had had their feet trimmed and were watching contently as Captain fought the farrier.

"Bye," he said gruffly as he took his check and stumbled into his car. Amanda stood soothing Captain for another few minutes before returning him to his stall.

"We waited a week and a half for that?!" Amanda said as she unclipped his lead.

"We'll find a better one next time. Hopefully Captain isn't to shaken," Liz replied. The farrier had yelled at all of them, but at Captain the most. The little Pindos had refused to stand still. Liz and Amanda had let him go in hopes that it would make him finish and leave quicker.

Yet Captain walked into his stall and sighed. He yawned and his stable mates snorted back.

"You stinkers!" Liz and Amanda said in unison. Captain was fine and had put on an act. He likes to annoy humans, and his pasture mates. But Liz and Amanda were happy the horses had done that, for they would've done the same thing. Liz watered, Amanda fed, and they skipped grooming for tonight. They felt like they had left the dogs out for a long time and wanted to spend tonight with them.

"Good boy, Bosco!" Liz said as the dog rolled over on the carpet. He'd already learned shake and speak, and Liz was very proud. Amanda played tug-of-war with Cassidy and Pepper; Bosco hadn't seemed interested in playing as a group. They played and taught the dogs' tricks for another hour before going to bed. The dogs stayed in the living room, while Liz and Amanda went to their bedrooms. The dogs were exhausted, and the humans were just as tired. Before the clock struck 9:30 they were all asleep.

∪∪∪

Liz battled the winds; she fought for every step. Bosco, Pepper, and Cassidy continued to play amongst themselves; the wind didn't seem to bother them. Liz's hands were frozen, and her nose and lips were numb. Amanda was in bed with a cold and sore throat, so Liz had had to do the chores on her own today. She jumped inside and shut the door. She took off her three layers of coats and sweaters before untying her shoes. She ran to the kitchen sink and ran her fingers under hot water.

"You would've been taken to the hospital if you'd gone outside today," Liz said to Amanda before they both started laughing. Amanda sat on the coach wrapped in blankets and sweaters, with a cup of tea in her hands. "Spring will be here before you know it," Amanda said, reaching for a tissue as she said it. Liz could only hope.

STEPS FORWARD

Angel brought her feet up and came around the ring at a beautiful park trot. Amanda stood in the middle and explained to Liz how she could improve. Liz slowed Angel to a walk and patted her neck.

"That was perfect!" Amanda jumped as she congratulated them.

"She felt great," Liz said, a little out of breath. "Walk on."

"We only need to work on her canter and she's good to go. But you still need to keep your back straight and center yourself in the saddle," Amanda explained with a laugh. Liz laughed too. Angel was always great and learned quick, but Liz needed a few lessons before she really got the hang of something.

Liz set the saddle in the tack room and groomed Angel. Amanda had just gone out to work with Captain and told Liz to work with Rocky. It was turning out to be a wonderful spring. Mud still covered most of the property and kept them from trail riding. Yet they continued training in the arena. They hoped to take showing more seriously this year.

"Rocky, stand," Liz said as the gelding pushed around. She clipped the lead to his halter and led him to the aisle. Liz slipped the end of the rope through the ring of the wall of the aisle, and went to get a brush. She brushed Rocky quickly and went back to the tack room. She lifted his heavy western saddle and balanced it best she could as she walked back. After cinching it up she had to fight him for a few minutes to get his bridle on.

"Com'on. It's not going to eat you. Good boy," Liz soothed. Rocky jogged out of the barn and up to the gait.

Liz watched Amanda get Captain used to the cart being on either side of him, while Rocky loped calmly around the ring. Rocky was ready for any Western competition, he was a "mutt" though, and wouldn't be allowed into many classes. Liz shifted her hand to the right and turned him in a circle and started in the other direction. He came to a jog and even turned his head to watch his friend. Captain rolled the whites of his eyes as the staffs of the cart touched his flanks, and moved up to his shoulders. Amanda soothed him and, once he relaxed the slightest bit, she slid the cart away from them. Captain sighed and Amanda led him around the ring. She brought him from a walk to a trot and back again a couple times before returning him to the barn.

"Jog on," Liz said. She tisked her tongue and Rocky picked up a smooth, relaxing jog.

"Trot," Liz gave the command and Rocky picked up a hunt seat trot: smooth, long, ground covering strides. Liz slowed him to the walk.

"Canter. Good boy," Liz said. Rocky started his rocking horse lope. If she wanted a hunt seat canter, she would ask him to go faster. Liz saw Amanda motion her in that it was enough for one day. Liz rode Rocky to the gate; she leaned over, unlatched it, and rode through. *Rocky would make a wonderful trail horse,* thought Liz.

After untacking and grooming Rocky, it was already time to start evening feeds. The days seem to go by too fast. Liz filled Penny's water bucket and dumped the rest in the muck pile. Amanda came walking up the aisle and kissed each horse on the nose. They turned out the light and went inside. Cassidy was already waiting on the porch.

"Have you seen Chalky?" Amanda asked as she looked around the house after dinner.

"No. You can't find him?" Liz asked. She wasn't too worried.

"I saw him a week ago, but I haven't since then," Amanda looked under the coach. "Chalky?" they shouted in unison. A meow came from the bedrooms upstairs. Amanda and Liz jumped and scrambled up the stairs, looking everywhere. Liz ran into Amanda's bedroom and searched the closet. She turned around to see Chalky at the foot of the bed.

"Chalky, come here," she said. Amanda was in the empty room down the hall and couldn't hear when Liz called. Chalky crawled under the bed, and more meowing came. Liz lifted the comforter that hung off the bed, and looked under.

"Amanda! Amanda! Come quick!" Liz screamed down the hall. Amanda flew into the room and looked under the bed with Liz. Chalky sat next to a brindle colored cat, kittens around their feet.

"Oh my God Chalky!" Amanda smiled. She lifted Chalky into her arms and kissed his forehead. The female cat came out from under the bed; the kittens followed her and meowed after their parents.

"You've been busy," Liz exclaimed. "Four kittens!"

There were two kittens that were Chalky's yellow color, one was a brindle, and the other was a brown kitten with white legs. Liz looked under the bed. A box that held some of Amanda's clothes looked like it had been the birthing nest. She pulled it out to find a kitten that hadn't made it. The female purred as it sat in Amanda's lap.

"Just throw out the clothes, this is better," she touched the female's soft fur. Liz brought it outside and hurried back in. Amanda had the kittens in the living room.

"What should we name the female," Amanda asked. They thought. It never crossed their minds that they couldn't keep the kittens.

"What about...?" They would continue with no name, for about a half an hour. The female seemed friendly, and the kittens were playful, Liz decided there was no reason why they couldn't stay.

"What about Jazz?" Liz finally said. "My father had a cat named Jazz. She was friendly, playful; it seems like a good name for her."

"I like that. Jazz... Jazz," Amanda stroked the cats back. "Welcome to your new home. You can raise your kittens, eat, and sleep."

OOO

Angel's powerful strides ate up the ground as they flew around the ring at a road trot. Liz laughed at Angel's enthusiasm. The Friesian was ready for competition at her own level: an all Friesian show.

"You're ready right, Angel?" Liz whispered as they continued their ride. Angel snorted, lifted her feet even higher, and trotted faster. Not missing a beat or losing her form.

READY?

Liz grabbed a handful of Angel's mane as she flew around the ring. Her trot was unbelievable: high in step, blinding speed, and in perfect form. It seemed like a natural gait for Angel now. Amanda cheered from the middle of the ring. Liz pulled gently on the reins, and after another, almost complete, lap around, Angel slowed to a walk.

"She just needs to get used to noises," Liz said as she brought Angel to the middle with Amanda.

"I guess you're right," Amanda stroked Angel's face. "Wanna start now? It's only the beginning of this lesson."

"Okay. Get some plastic bags, or something that makes noise. I'll just walk her around the arena," Liz said before Amanda started toward the house.

Amanda returned with a metal cookie sheet, three plastic bags, and her shouting voice. She tied the bags to the rails of the arena, and would shout and bang on the cookie sheet with a large cooking spoon. Angel jumped and whirled at the sounds.

"Easy. It's okay. Walk on," Liz stayed calm and Angel started to do the same. After seven minutes, the only thing Angel wasn't comfortable with yet, was the bags.

"Whooooooooaaaaaaaa!!!" Amanda shouted as she walked around the outside. Angel paid her no mind and watched the bag she was about to pass. It made a noise as the wind lifted it, and the mare jumped sideways.

Liz realized more and more each day, just how big this mare was. At almost 16 hands she was very big. Angel half bolted into a trot to pass the bag the rest of the way. After four or five laps, at just a walk, Liz brought Angel to the barn.

"That was great!" Amanda said before drinking from her water bottle. Angel rubbed her itchy head against Liz's shoulder, nearly pushing her to the floor.

"We just need to update her a little bit more," Amanda said.

"What?" Liz asked, puzzled.

"She needs her coggins renewed, her weight and height taken again. She'll be six in April sometime," Amanda explained as she helped Liz carry the tack to the tack room.

"Her feet are trimmed so we won't half to worry about that for another month or so. Thank God!" Liz added as she remembered the blacksmith that had come. All of a sudden, Chalky, Jazz and their kittens came running down the aisle. The kittens meowed and hissed at each other playfully. They had to be at least four weeks old by the way they were acting and looking. Liz picked up Jazz and the cat purred with delight.

Liz and Amanda made their way to the house. Chalky and Jazz had made a nest in the feed room; using old towels and rags. But the dogs followed them into the house and ran to eat from their feed dishes. Amanda and Liz watched and laughed.

"I think there's some kind of Friesian event going on next week," Amanda said.

"Oh. Well you would have to place us in a class. I'm not too educated about the showing stuff," Liz explained.

They heated up leftover spaghetti, and sat at the kitchen table to eat it.

"Well, she'd be great in a road hack class. It's where they walk, trot, road trot, canter and gallop," Amanda took a bite of her spaghetti. "And she'd have to stay in form while she does all the gaits. Or she could participate in a classic pleasure class where she has to walk, trot, park or road trot, and canter."

"Well. I think she'd have more fun doing the road hack class," Liz smiled.

Angel's hoof beats pounded in Liz's ears. They flew around the arena at a blinding speed, passing the other Friesians, one by one. They were called to the line up and the judge checked over each horse.

"First Place goes to Guardian Angel!" the loudspeaker boomed their name. Liz nearly cried. Ribbons and a blanket of flowers were placed on Angel's bridle and withers. The spotlight lit the ring, the moon seemed to smile, the crowd cheering was endless, and thousands of pictures must've been taken in that moment. Angel snorted and stood in her show ring position.

When it came time for her victory lap, Angel, who was bursting with energy and pride, bolted to the rail at a head spinning park trot. The more she trotted the faster she seemed to go. Angel's snorts and hoof beats sounded like music; Liz loved it. Then, the crowds seem to fade like morning mist, their cheering went with them. The moon became the sun; the camera flashes became its rays. Liz looked around, bewildered. They were in the field! She sat bareback on Angel; the bridle seemed to be the only "unwild" object around them.

Liz woke with a jolt at the sound of her alarm clock. Bosco whined and left the room. Its screeching beeps went on for a minute before Liz was able to find the switch. With four days until the show, Liz got up early every morning to take extra care of Angel. She started the coffee pot, started some "Easy Oven" muffins and then brought half a dozen carrots to the barn. She would finish feeds and everything without Amanda today. Amanda was exhausted, she had been going non-stop and Liz wouldn't wake her up. She had slept through her own alarm and Liz's, so she wouldn't be getting up soon.

"Let's go guys," Liz said as the dogs jumped around her feet. The horses whinnied from the barn and the dogs barked back.

Liz gave everybody grain before throwing a few flakes of hay out in the pasture and leading them out. She let Angel out as well, and mucked out the small clumps of soiled shavings. Liz gave the aisle a quick light sweeping and went back to the house. Amanda was just walking down the steps and was still rubbing her eyes.

"How could you let me sleep 'til 9:00?" Amanda was a little annoyed and looked at Liz with a questioning eye.

"You needed the sleep. I did the chores and put everybody out in the pasture. We can exercise them later. It's not that late anyways," Liz explained as she poured two cups of coffee.

""Well, I don't think she needs it," Amanda smiled at Liz.

"What?" Liz spun around so quickly that the coffee almost flew from the cups she was holding. Liz thought they would still be cramming in lessons until the show.

"I would just lounge her at the gaits, give her a bath or two, brush her, and make sure you don't do anything to loose her bond with you," Amanda explained as she took a sip of her coffee.

"Really?" Liz questioned once more.

"Yeah. You guys look great together. You'll both be fine," Amanda assured her. They drank their coffee and discussed what might happen. They also told each other to never get into the "what ifs" when showing.

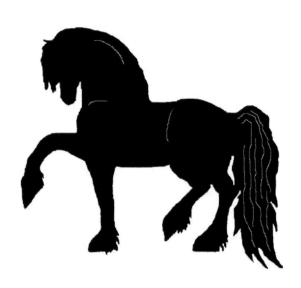

HOW'D THAT HAPPEN

The show grounds bustled with activity. Friesians of all sizes were led around, exercised, and fed. Angel jumped about, taking in everything. Amanda had laid down bedding and feed in the stall they'd rented, and Liz led her hyper mare to the barn.

"Right here," Amanda pointed to a stall in the middle. They had an extra stall for supplies. They left Angel in the stall and unpacked everything they needed from the trailer.

"Go get the number, and I'll make sure Angel doesn't get into any trouble," Liz smiled as they parted ways at the trailer. Liz made her way slowly and carefully back to the barn.

When she arrived, Liz found almost a dozen people gathered around Angel's stall. The mare looked at them with startled eyes.

"Excuse me," Liz said as she made her way into the stall. Angel came up and looked for treats.

"She's amazing!"

"Where'd you get her?"

"What's her breeding?"

Liz looked around to see the people asking questions and examining Angel with such enthusiasm.

"Oh," Liz said. She didn't know what to say. "Well. Her sire is Black Everest. And her dam is Netel Violet." Amanda came around the corner holding a folder. She stopped in her tracks and gestured to Liz "What's going on?" Liz shrugged; she'd never been to a show, she didn't know what this was about. Amanda joined the crowd outside the stall and helped answer questions.

Angel snorted and bobbed her head; revealing the ivory star between her eyes. People hesitated, before continuing to ask questions.

"Who cares if you have a star? Cause you're going to be one soon," Liz comforted Angel. As the people started to drift away, Amanda, Liz, and Angel started settling in. They rented a small camper on the grounds and got ready for the next day.

Liz made finishing touches to her appearance before meeting Amanda outside. Angel was polished and warmed up; she danced around ready to get going on the job.

"Class 22, Road Hack. Entries, please be ready, we are moments away!" the announcer made it clear.

"I'll walk you guys to the ring," Amanda said as she noticed Liz's nervousness. Angel's forelock was pushed away, showing off her large star.

"Let's show 'em!" Liz encouraged both herself and Angel.

They were the third in the arena. Angel's powerful strides made her soar over the ground. She heard people make comments and saw them point.

"Good girl," Liz assured the mare. Some of the Friesians had ribbons in their manes, but Angel's looked natural.

"Trot!" came the command, as the gaits were closed. *This is it!*, Liz thought.

When it was time, Angel's canter was magnificent. Liz barely had to do anything. Every time she passed in front of the judge, people from all over would scream and holler. Liz felt great, and Angel did too.

"Reverse!" Angel slowed to a walk and turned to go in the other direction.

"Good girl. Easy," Liz said as she caught her breath.

"Trot! Trot, Please!" the command boomed through the speaker. Angel didn't need to be told; her heart seemed to rest in her legs and hooves the way she moved. Three times around the large, outdoor arena, and they called the canter.

It took a moment, but Angel found her stride and felt like a rocking horse as she glided around the arena.

"To the center!" Liz slowed Angel to a fast trot, and pulled her next to another Friesian. Angel looked magnificent; satin, ebony coat rippling over her toned muscles, head high, ears alert. As the judge walked down, he inspected each with a careful eye. He made his way to a stallion and the crowd gave an uproar of approval; they did so for two others. Liz was last out of the thirteen teams that were in the arena. The judge came to stand in front of Angel, the big mare stood picture perfect. The crowd gave another uproar, even though the star on her forehead shone bright against her black coat.

"Very nice," he congratulated. He walked away and Liz murmured to Angel.

"And the results!" the announcer got everyone excited. "In first place…" the name was sounded and the stallion down the line trotted out to receive a bright blue ribbon. As did another stallion for second.

"Guardian Angel and Liz Parker for third!" Liz's mouth went agape. Angel knew her name and strutted forth to have a yellow ribbon placed on her bridle. The crowd cheered, clapped and smiled as Angel left the arena. Liz hugged Angel as Amanda pushed her way from the stands to greet them.

"I can't believe it!" Liz said. She polished her boots and set them aside. It was almost an hour after the class. They planned to stay until tomorrow afternoon to watch some classes.

"She was fantastic. I don't know why everyone was gathered over here. I mean she's beautiful and all, but her parents were hacks," Amanda said with a frown. Hacks meant they were training buddies or just used for a little breeding then sold from owner to owner.

"Don't know," Liz shrugged. She went into Angel's stall and braided her mane for no reason at all. "You were great out there." Angel let her eyes droop as she readied herself for sleep.

"Is the owner of Guardian Angel in this barn?!" a man yelled from the barn door.

"Right here!" Amanda pointed into Angel's stall. The man hurried up to them. He walked with a limp, but made his way to them quite quickly.

"Congratulations! Here is your prize money," He handed them an envelope. "And you placed in the top three so you are immediately accepted to the finals tomorrow. Class 82, arena A. Good luck"

"Okay," Liz answered a little startled. She opened the folder that held information for the class. Liz and Amanda high fived each other and both ran to hug Angel. They turned and stared at each other.

"How'd that happen?!" they said in unison. Angel shook her head and snorted.

A DREAM COME TRUE

Liz watched as the crowds faded and she was lost in the field. She sat bare back on Angel. The mare lifted her head into the wind and took a deep breath. Liz laughed and hugged Angel's muscular neck.

"Ready? I think you should warm her up on your own," Amanda said. She gave Liz a leg into the saddle. Angel took off toward the arena they'd been in last night. "We need to go somewhere else tonight," Liz smiled. And it was true; it was 6:35. Liz steered Angel into the arena next to A. Angel trotted around just as nicely as she had the other day. She snorted and tossed her head. "Easy," Liz soothed as she started to feel Angel ready herself to gallop. Liz grabbed a small handful of mane as Angel bolted into a road trot. People came up and lined the rail to watch. They gave her words of wisdom and encouragement. Liz nodded and smiled, she only heard half of what she was told as she whirled down the rail. Yesterday hadn't had the smallest effect on Angel.

All of a sudden, Liz saw why people admired her the way they did. She was broad and muscled for a mare. Her head and neck was also wide for a mare; she could be calm and quiet, then bold and excited.

"Liz! Let her gallop a few strides!" Amanda called from the center of the arena.

Angel strutted her stuff as they waited for a free spot to get into the arena. As a spot opened that was just big enough for Angel to squeeze through, the mare bolted. Liz grabbed a handful of mane. They settled into rhythm on the rail.

"Easy," Liz soothed, as Angel got ready to go faster.

"And on at the trot!" Liz had everything she could do to keep Angel from braking stride into her flashy road trot. Angel passed in front of the judge and the crowd roared. Angel lifted her head and knees higher as she got encouragement from the fans. Her forelock flapped from her forehead as she paraded down the rail. People gasped and pointed. She passed the judge again and the crowd cheered, whistled and clapped. Liz smiled from ear to ear and even started to laugh.

"Take it to the Road Trot!" the announcer said above the roar of the crowd. Angel flew into action without missing a beat. She passed one, two, three horses. She whirled by the judge and the crowd went crazy. Angel kept her form; Liz wondered if Angel even needed her as she continued to strut her stuff. They passed the judge and they got the same reaction.

"Canter please!" Angel gladly went into her flashy rocking horse canter. She was so beautiful. Only two laps around and Angel was ready for a gallop.

"Hand Gallop please!" the command came as if on cue. Angel blasted forward. Liz grabbed a handful of mane and the crowd roared as they passed in front of the judge. The Friesian mare made her way around the big outdoor arena at a flying gallop, all the while stepping high, neck arched, nose in; perfect.

After they galloped, they had to walk, then halt and stand for a moment. Angel didn't like this part. She bobbed her head and gave short snorts.

"Easy. Stand, we'll be done in a minute," Liz explained to the excited mare.

"Canter!" the announcer said it in a mumble, and it took everyone a minute to realize the command. Angel jumped forward; it took almost seven strides before she found her pace with the help of Liz. The judge eyed each horse carefully; the crowd roared for Liz and the stallion that had won yesterday. They started to gallop as the command came twice.

"Looking great!" Amanda shouted, as Angel and Liz passed by. Liz couldn't stop laughing. Two laps around and the command came to trot.

"Trot. Good girl, easy," Liz talked to Angel as she tried to break into a gallop. Angel high stepped with all her might around the arena. She passed the judge and the crowd gave another uproar. Liz fell forward a little because she was laughing so hard. The road trot came and was long. Angel didn't seem to think it was though, she kept going without slowing or breaking stride.

"Come to the line up!" the announcement came at last.

"Stand," Liz said as they came forward. The crowd continued to roar and applaud until the judge got a good distance away.

"Results will be momentarily!" the announcement was exciting. Angel backed a step, and then let her head hang a little. Liz knew she was tired and the judging was over, so she didn't correct the mare's form.

"We have the results for class 82, Road Hack Championship," he waited a moment. All five horses had lost their form in tiredness. "Fifth..., Fourth..., Third...,"the announcements didn't call Angel's name and Liz got nervous and excited.

"And we are going to announce the reserve champion first. The Reserve Champion of the Road Hack Championship... is Guardian Angel and Liz Parker!" the crowd's roar drowned out Liz's name and she was glad. She had barely done anything. They wrapped the red and yellow ribbons around Angel's broad neck; a smaller one was hooked to her bridle.

The champion was announced. Before doing his victory lap, he made room for Angel. She pranced outside the ring, waiting eagerly and wanting to show off.

"Guardian Angel!!!" the announcer called them into the arena. It was pitch black; the spotlight followed them and showed the crowd the real winner. Angel roared around the arena, the crowd cheered, whistled, clapped and hollered. Angel and Liz made two extra laps; the last class of the night and it seemed okay. Camera flashes came from all directions, thousands it seemed like. Liz grabbed Angel's mane and almost let the reins completely go. Angel whinnied and trotted so fast the spotlight seemed to fall behind.

ᴜᴜᴜ

Angel breathed quietly as she walked along the trails. Liz closed her eyes and took everything in. The wind lifted Angel's mane and tail and she really did seem like an angel. She trotted quietly along the narrow path; her trot was mellow and her hoof beats subtle. Liz knew that the crowd at the horseshow had loved them and they didn't need a champion ribbon to show that. The crowd had loved her.

"The judge probably put you in that place because of her star. Some people are like that," Amanda had explained. Now on the trail alone, they felt free. Liz had put a buckle blanket on but no saddle. Angel was free and Liz let her go wherever the Friesian mare felt like.

ᴜᴜᴜ

"You are the only champion Angel. Around here you're the queen," Liz told the mare as she flipped an ear back. The mare listened intently like the smart horse she was. Angel would always be there. Always be there to be smart, caring, loving, and ready to strut her stuff whenever she needed or wanted to. Liz knew whatever lay ahead, even if no one else was there, Angel would be. Guardian Angel lived up to her name, and always would.

DREAMS...

Dear Reader,
    Thank you for reading my very first book. I had a great time writing it and I hope you enjoyed reading it just as much. I must let you know, especially if you found interest in my writing, the adventures will continue!
    May you always share happiness and friendship in all of your days…

Dream Always,
Ashley

P. S. - I chose the Friesian horse, as a dedication to my "Aunt Liz". If you would like to see all of the beautiful and magnificent Morgan horses that I spoil each and every day, please visit us all at:

www.TripleSweetMorgans.com.

Direct Inquiries to:

TripleSweetMorgans@hotmail.com
www.TripleSweetMorgans.com

GUARDIAN ANGEL